# Ticket to Her Heart

Rocky Mountain Christmas Train

## Rocky Mountain Christmas Train
### Book Six

## Katie O'Connor

Snarky Heart Press

# Ticket
## to
# Her Heart

Rocky Mountain Christmas Train
Book Six

Katie O'Connor

—Ticket to Her Heart—
—The Rocky Mountain Christmas Train: Book Six—

This book is a work of fiction. Names, characters, places, and incidents either are products of the author's imagination or are used fictitiously. Any resemblance to actual events, locales, or persons, living or dead, is entirely coincidental.

Published November 2024 by Snarky Heart Press and Katie O'Connor
(katieohwrites.com)

ISBN: 978-1-989816-88-2 Digital Edition 1

ISBN: 978-1-989816-90-5 Digital Edition 2

ISBN: 978-1-989816-92-9  (Print Edition)

Cover art by Kelly Moran
Copyediting by Terri St. Clair

## Dedication

For everyone who loves trains, romance, snow, or
Christmas. You are my people.
Thanks to my dedicated friends and fans.

# About This Book

Madeline Hayes has been through a lot in her life but this trip on the Rocky Mountain Christmas train might just be the most entertaining, and the most stressful thing she's ever done. But she wouldn't trade it for anything.

She's alive in a way she's never felt before because she's finally met the man of her dreams. She's hoping he loves her back and that his love is strong enough to see past her necessary lies and into her heart.

Are there too many barriers in their way for a romance to blossom? Will her secret keep them apart? Or will the magic of Christmas help them overcome their differences to find love?

## Chapter One

Madeline Hayes gathered up a few scraps of wrapping paper and stuffed it into the garbage. She plopped into Santa's abandoned leather chair in the rear observation car and sighed as The Rocky Mountain Christmas Train rolled out of Canmore toward its second last stop. The twenty-four-day journey would end in Rocky Mountain House, Alberta, in only two days. One lucky person would win twenty-five thousand dollars for the charity of their choice on Christmas Eve.

Melancholy washed over her. She'd adored the people she was working with and was going to miss them. She'd made friends that would last a lifetime...if her lies didn't ruin those friendships. For the hundredth time, she wondered if there might have been another way to meet her goal. This trip was the beginning of a whole new way of living, and as far as she managed to figure out, the lies were her the only way to achieve her life-changing goal.

Though she was alone in the car, Maddie hid her frown. She had a facade to maintain and couldn't risk anyone seeing her worries. It wasn't her job to tidy up, the train had staff for that, but she couldn't help herself.

She'd been hired to play the role of nurse to Christopher Watson; the private investigator who vetted the contestants and was keeping track of their antics. Nobody, not even Chris, knew she had massive secrets. Friendship ending secrets.

Lying didn't come easy, but in this case, it was absolutely necessary. She couldn't see any way around it. So far, it was working out fine. Nobody seemed to suspect her of duplicity and this trip and the year of research leading up to it had been wonderful.

When this trip was over, she would miss her 'patient' Chris most of all. He was fun, intelligent, kind, and outgoing. He did his job well and kept up the disguise of an old man without once slipping up. He was aboard to protect the interests of the trip's benefactor.

There was a lot at stake for the benefactor and the potential winning charities. Twenty-five thousand dollars could make people do strange or unethical things. That meant a distinct possibility of shenanigans and outright cheating by the contestants. Six teams had been removed from the train for cheating. Hopefully, there won't be more. Her heart ached for the charities that were no longer in line for funding because their contestants broke the rules. And they had done so willingly, in front of a massive and growing audience who were eager for daily updates.

The private train's inaugural ride and the start of the contest had generated enormous media attention. Television and radio newscasters and bloggers met them at every stop looking for updates. The increased traffic to the towns along the way brought tourist dollars for an economic boost.

With an initial one hundred people paired into fifty teams, there were only two duos left to compete. Four teams had failed to execute their assigned tasks but were still on the train. Having put in honest efforts, the contest's benefactor had allowed them to complete the trip without further penalty and at no cost.

Excitement trilled through her. One more stop and then onto their final destination. So much could happen in two days. Watching the contestants was fun, but observing their interactions, good and bad, was fascinating. She was learning more about how people got along, or didn't, than she had imagined. This trip was, to say the very least, enlightening. What surprised her most was how all the teams cheered on their competitors and became friends.

The train was stopped for the night and light snow drifted past the windows. The beauty was unparalleled by anything she'd ever seen. It snowed at home in New York City, but there was something about fresh snow in the mountains that was beautiful and invigorating, even from inside the train. The colored Christmas lights gave the snow a magical glow that felt like a good omen.

Jenny, the train's hostess and emcee, still wearing her official Mrs. Claus costume, came into the car and flopped down onto a sturdy red chair with a heavy sigh. "Golly, what I wouldn't give for a double shot of tequila right now."

"Boy, do I feel that! I'm beyond exhausted. But rules are rules." She sat down near her friend.

"I didn't think a month of sobriety would be this hard." Jenny swept her frilly white cap off her head and tossed it onto the sofa.

Next to Chris, Jenny was the hardest person to lie to. She was kind and generous, and rapidly becoming a close friend. Working together had turned strangers into close friends.

The trip was a blast, but some days were stressful. Jenny was an easy confidante. Still, more than once, Maddie had been headed for the bar car and a good stiff drink to calm her nerves or soothe her guilt over her lies. Luckily, Cliff and Bruce, the main bar staff members, had become good friends and had calmed her down.

"I had no idea how hard it would be. At least we had the illusion of drinking." Maddie laughed.

"You know, I thought the idea of having mocktails instead of true cocktails, if invited by guests to join them, was ridiculous," Jenny confessed. "But I've lost track of how many frustrated and disappointed contestants I've had 'drinks' with. So many people dating and then breaking up. I guess Christmas romances aren't like they appear in the movies."

"True. And the contestants who failed out despite their best efforts? Those are the folks I feel the worst for." She had commiserated with the less successful candidates. Some could relax and enjoy the rest of their trip, but others were moping. And who could blame them?

Jenny poured herself a cocoa from the carafe on the side counter. "Want one?"

"I swear if I drink another cocoa before next Christmas, it'll be too soon."

"Come on, get into the holiday spirit. It's almost Christmas Eve and the end of the trip. One more stop and the announcement of the winning team and charity. I can't wait to see who wins. And if I'm honest, to get some rest."

"Me too. Three weeks without a day off is a long time." She was looking forward to the rest, but not to the end of her time with Christopher. Unlike many of the contestants, their friendship probably wouldn't continue after the trip because when he found out the depth of her secret, he'd run as fast as his legs would carry him. After watching one team cheat and lie, he'd confided that there was nothing he despised more than a liar. She suspected there was a personal story in his adamant belief, but he had yet to share it with her.

She stood and stretched away the ache in her lower back. "I guess I better go tuck my patient in for the night and get to bed. Tomorrow's coming like a freight train."

"Nice wordplay. Catch you later." Jenny leaned back. "Don't forget his nightly salted caramel hot cocoa."

"As if he'd let me." How Chris could continue to drink the stuff confounded her. She shuddered just thinking about more cocoa...of any flavor. "Note to self: bring more tea next time."

Jenny laughed at the quip.

Maddie was tired of the train's limited selection of tea. She needed something more, like the expensive blend she drank at home. "Poor planning on your part, Maddie. Do better." She prepped the cocoa and repeated, 'Bring more tea' to her growing mental list of things to do. She found it helped to say them aloud. It was as if hearing the words locked them into her memory.

Staff quarters were scattered among the passenger cars. The employee accommodations were much less luxurious than their special guests but still very nice. With the passengers believing that Christopher was a wealthy old man, and she his nurse, they had been assigned better suites than the contestants and the other staff. Their adjoining suites were top-end passenger cabins.

She strode through the last twelve of fifty cars, stepping carefully through the connecting accordion fold protectors between cars lest she spill Chris's nightly beverage. Each car was decorated for the holidays with lights and ornaments, and during the daytime, there was soft Christmas music playing. Everything from instrumental to current hits to the classics. Finally, she reached their adjoining suites. She tapped her keycard against her lock and entered the private sanctuary that was her room.

She glanced around the forest green and cream decor. With a variety of color schemes available, she was pleased to end up with this warm combination. The room's calming colors were soothing enough that she'd taken a dozen pictures. She intended to redo her bedroom at home in matching colors. Unless she moved.

She adored the Santa throw pillows on her bed and chair. They reminded her of her one happy Christmas with her paternal grandmother. Nanna was the only person in her family she missed. Nanna loved Christmas.

Maddie's bed had been made since she left her room at eight that morning. The train staff was both efficient and unobtrusive. Much more so than those in the luxury lodges she'd once visited with her parents. She'd seen a lot in her thirty-six years, but this train trip was unique. It combined fun, elegance, the holidays, and the finest staff she'd ever encountered.

Setting Chris's cocoa on the table that served as her desk, she tossed her bag onto the bed. Kicking her shoes under the comfy chair in the corner, she sat down with a sigh of relief and leaned back to admire the elegant holiday decor of her room. So many details were taken care of - from the tiny tree on the desk to the glittering stars hanging in the windows reflecting the colorful lights hanging outside her window. She loved Christmas and all its trappings. Food, music, decorations, and giving gifts filled her heart with the joy she thought she'd never have again. She hadn't been this happy since she was twelve.

The door to Chris's adjoining room was ajar.

"Chris," she called softly, "are you still up?"

"Ya." His voice was a grunt.

Oh no. He sounded grumpy. He had to be frustrated with the role he played. An active, able-bodied man stuck in a wheelchair for three weeks, he was probably going stir crazy. Generally, he took it in stride. Mostly because he was being paid very well for his services as a P.I.

She picked up his drink and walked, sock-footed, into the room which mirrored hers. She expected to see him typing away on his laptop. After his days of rolling around 'spying' on the contestants, he put in long hours in his suite, summarizing his observations.

He was not at his desk.

He had his legs hooked over a bar hanging from the bathroom door and was doing inverted sit-ups. His chest and ab muscles flexed and pulled with each grunting motion. *Sweet heavenly Christmas.*

She knew he was fit, but holy Yule logs, he was buff in the extreme. Like totally lean and tight and drool-worthy.

*Bank it, Maddie. He's not for you. Don't let on that you think he's as hot as sin. Go about your life and forget about him.*

He paused, upside down, and stared at her, his dark brown eyes shining. "Is that my cocoa?"

She swallowed back a lump of fiery attraction. "Yes."

He pulled back up, gripped the bar, flipped over backward onto his feet, and held out his hand. His damp cocoa-brown hair spiked up in all directions. "Thanks. I love this stuff."

She slipped the heavy mug and saucer into his outstretched fingers. "I brought you some coconut macaroons, too."

His grin melted her heart. "You spoil me."

"It's the least I can do with you being trapped inside this room unless you're in that chair." And it assuaged the guilt in her heart. Taking a few extra minutes to be nice to him made her happy. She loved caring for other people. It was why she became a nurse.

"I get out now and then." He bit off a huge chunk of cookie. Good thing she'd brought four of them. He ate like he was starving.

"You don't get out often enough."

His shrug was as eloquent. "I'm having a blast. People have no idea that I'm not even forty. It's fun pretending to be an old war veteran with a hot nurse."

Heat flooded her face. She had no idea he'd even looked closely at her. Sure, they were developing a close friendship and confiding a lot in each other, but this was the first time he'd admitted any attraction.

"I...I don't think we're supposed to fraternize with the other staff." Great. Way to sound lame, Maddie. He's going to think you're the biggest wimp. She stared out the window at the falling snow.

"Doesn't matter to me if it doesn't matter to you." His low, sexy tone drew her attention back to him and fueled the heat in her cheeks.

His smile was pure sin, and she was sorely tempted to see if he was for real or just teasing. She pretended to consider the idea. "I think I'll pass and not take the risk of losing my job."

"Your loss." He winked. "But if you change your mind, you know where to find me."

"I do indeed." And didn't she wish she could slip into his embrace for a kiss?

"You know, we could both leave the train. The contest is all but finished..."

The innuendo in his voice should have made her uncomfortable. It would have if it came from another man. But from Chris, with all she knew about him, it was just flirting. A fun game between them. It was a new side of him. They had never flirted, and she liked the flutters it set off in her belly.

"If I change my mind, you'll be the first to know." She paused. Then, in keeping with the character she was playing, she added, "This is my first gig as a private nurse." True, as far as it went. "I'm hoping for a good reference when this is done."

"Come on, Maddie. This is fake. One hundred percent. You know it. I know it. Our mysterious boss and benefactor of this whole ridiculous contest knows it."

"You think it's ridiculous that people have the chance to win twenty-five thousand dollars for charity? I think it's brilliant." She crossed her arms over her chest.

"Brilliant? What does it cost to have a hundred people on a train for three weeks? What about staff, food, stops, and the expenses of side excursions? Travel to get everyone to the train and home again. The person behind this would have made a bigger impact if they just flat-out donated to charity. I question their motivation in spending this massive sum instead of just giving it. What does it accomplish?"

She stared at him. "Don't you see the good the contest is doing? It reunited people who were torn from loved ones. Just look at Team T-Rex. It brought Tracy and Rex back together after a decade apart. It's heartwarming." She shook her head. "It's brought new hearts together in love, like Seth and Joy of Team Triple Threat. Look at how happy Joy's daughter, Chantal, is with her new relationship with Seth. Besides, it's fun, it earns recognition for all the named charities. Many of them are reporting increased donations."

"Who told you that?" He narrowed his eyes and stared at her while he finished his second cookie. "Do you know the benefactor?"

"We've met." She swallowed a lump of self-reprisal for the slight fabrication.

His mouth dropped open, spilling crumbs all over the carpeting. She pushed his mouth shut with the tip of her finger and tried not to think about the prickle of his five o'clock shadow under her fingers.

"What?" She shrugged and gave him an innocent look that further grated on her conscience. "They swore me to secrecy. Pretend I didn't mention it." She put her hands together like she was praying and begged, "Please. I could lose my job over letting it slip." Another lie. They were stacking up like flapjacks at a Sunday brunch.

His glare could have bored through concrete. "I thought we were friends. I thought maybe we were even—" He snapped his mouth shut.

"Even what?" Could he be feeling something for her? Like she was feeling for him? She swallowed a hopeful yearning.

"Nothing. Just nothing. I think you should go." He glared at the door as if his gaze could push her back to her side. His hand was white knuckled on the plate he still held. "Goodnight, Maddie."

"Goodnight, Chris." She backed into her room and shut the door. The second door between their suites slammed shut. The deadbolt clicked home with a loud thunk.

Her heart dropped to her toes. He'd never locked the connecting door before.

Now she'd done it.

Ruined any chance she had with him. She should have known better than to get her hopes up.

If he was this upset over a simple secret, how would he feel when he learned the breadth of her actual lies? If that tiny evasion had made him furious, she was doomed. Her eyes burned and her chest ached. She gasped and wrapped her arms around her waist.

"Why did you have to fall for him?" she whispered, dashing away a tear. "You went your whole life without connecting to anyone but Nanna. Not even your parents. Now you had to go and fall for the exact person you could never have."

Katie O'Connor

## Chapter Two

Morning came too early for Chris. His head pounded like he had a three-alarm hangover.

"Ha. You wish. If you'd drank yourself into oblivion, you'd feel better." Instead, he'd stayed awake, fuming over Maddie's deception. They'd been together on this stupid train for twenty-two days. Just over three weeks. And not once had she mentioned knowing who their benefactor was. They'd discussed it at least a dozen times. Probably more. They'd spent hours debating who it might be and what their motivation for the contest was.

He popped a couple of pills for his aching head and climbed into his costume, carefully gluing his beard to his face. He was not going to miss using spirit gum, that's for sure. She knocked right on time. Honestly, he was half tempted to ignore her or send her on her way. Unfortunately, he was starving.

Maybe he should just order room service.

His ethics drove him to discard the idea. He was being paid to supervise the contestants and he couldn't do that locked in his luxurious suite.

"Chris? Are you up yet?" she asked in her annoyingly perky morning voice.

"Come in."

She jiggled the door handle. "It's locked."

Crap. He'd forgotten he locked her out last night. He stomped to the door and flung it open.

"Good morning and Merry Christmas." Her smile was bright and wide. Her blonde hair was pulled up in a messy bun he wanted to take out. He loved her long golden locks.

"Bah humbug."

"Oh, come on, Christopher. It's a beautiful sunny morning. We've got the entire day to ourselves. Nothing to do but relax. There are only two tasks left on the docket and they take place on the train. You should be happy. Your job is almost done."

"I'll be glad to be away from here."

She looked up at him. Her expression was serious, her eyes pained and shadowed. "Look, Christopher. I'm sorry I didn't tell you. Maybe I should have. I probably should have. But I have no way to go back and change things. I can't undo not telling you. At least now you know."

"Any other dirty little secrets?" People who lied once usually lied twice. Some made it a habit. His ex-wife had turned out to be a habitual liar. Some days he swore that when June opened her mouth she was lying.

"Are there things about me that I haven't told you? Yes. But I'm sure there are things I don't know about you too." She swallowed audibly. "I'd like to think that those things will come out as our friendship develops." Her purse handle squeaked beneath her fingers.

He grunted. Someday he'd have to tell her about his ex-partner and his ex-wife. If he forgave her. "Honesty is important to me, Maddie. More than you know."

"And to me as well. Three things I value in people are honesty, kindness, and the generosity to help others." She shuffled her feet. "Truthfully, I wasn't always kind or generous. There was a time when I was rather nasty. I'm ashamed to admit that I was a hideous person."

The shame in her voice was almost visible. He couldn't imagine her being hideous, not on the outside, or on the inside. She was sunny and upbeat. Helpful and kind. She was the antithesis of a nasty person. "I find that hard to believe."

"Believe me. You would not have liked the person I was just six years ago. Before I turned over a new leaf and went into nursing."

"What changed you?"

"That's a question for another day. The explanation is long and ugly. I'd prefer to get through this trip without sullying it with details of my sordid past. I'm asking you to trust that eventually, you'll know everything about me." She shuffled to the door with slouched shoulders and turned back to look him in the eye. "I swear it. I promise to tell you about my entire life. After this trip is finished, I'll answer every question you ask."

He walked over and looked down at her. She barely came up to his chin. The sorrowful look in her blue eyes didn't match the frolicking elves on her rich green sweater or her light floral scent. He'd never be able to smell lobelia and marigolds without thinking of her. The dichotomy between her current expression and her usual smile pained him. He'd grown accustomed to the upbeat Maddie, not this beaten, defeated, pale imitation of her.

He couldn't find it in his heart to forgive her mistake. Forgiveness wasn't easy for him. He could try to give her the benefit of the doubt. Going forward, she would have to prove her honesty. He pulled his wheelchair out of the corner and took a seat after straightening his wig and checking his makeup was still intact.

"Shall we get breakfast?"

Her smile brightened a hundred watts. "Absolutely. It'll be my pleasure."

Working together, they rolled the chair to the dining room, where the introduction of today's contests was scheduled to take place. Over the past weeks, the morning event had switched between the forward observation lounge, the dining room, and the library car. It was announced the evening before where the event would be held. However, the contestants rarely learned more than an hour or two in advance that it was their turn. Each morning, in the wee hours, an envelope was slipped beneath the contestants' doors, inviting them to come to take part.

"Is this good?" she asked as she slid his chair into an empty space near the back of the room.

"Perfect," he grumbled in his old man's voice. "I can nearly see."

"Good morning, Mr. Chris," Chantal Spencer greeted him. "Morning, Miss Maddie. Are you ready for Christmas? Santa is going to bring me something special this year." She braced herself on her arm crutches, leaned in close, and whispered, "I think he's bringing me a dad." She giggled. Her mother Joy had been paired up with Seth Mathison early in the trip and it looked like they were on the fast track to a serious relationship.

"I'll be hoping you get what you want." Chris grinned. "Mr. Mathison is a nice man."

"Yup." She leaned in and gave him a wobbly hug. "Can we play cards again later?"

"You better believe it."

"Yay." She waved one hand without releasing her crutches and walked slowly down the row to where her mother sat holding hands with her new beau.

"I didn't know you were playing cards with her," Maddie said. "When did you find time for that?"

"Almost every day, while you're off on your afternoon break." Doing whatever it was she needed an hour a day to complete. Up until last night, he'd believed she was doing paperwork on the day's events and who they'd been watching. Basically, he assumed she'd been doing what he did every evening after he 'retired' for the night.

"You are such a sweet man."

"I'm crotchety and old," he complained for the benefit of those sitting nearby.

She leaned in and kissed his cheek. "Keep telling yourself that, Mr. Watson. I know better."

He barely restrained from reaching up to touch his cheek above his beard where her lips had brushed. He'd dreamed of kissing her for weeks. No, longer than that. They had met a full year before the start of their journey. They'd worked together researching the contestants.

He had vetted and investigated every contestant, with Maddie's help. The contest was open to applicants from Canada and the United States, which accounted for tens of thousands of applicants.

Some had been chosen from their applications, others through an advice column called Ask Ginny which had been set up as a way to find worthy people, people with problems that could be solved by winning or by participating. One contestant had gotten over her fear of dogs while helping a local train his sled dogs.

How the final contestants were chosen, he had no idea. He investigated for a criminal past, generosity, kindness, and a few other specific traits. Each charity was vetted as well. He compiled a list of acceptable contestants, and the benefactor selected the final one hundred.

Some contestants had come in with well-known charities, and others with more personal reasons for entering.

Chantal's mother needed the money to pay off their enormous medical debts, with the rest going to the Cerebral Palsy Association. There were requests for funds to open dance and karate schools. Requests to fund education and animal care shelters were common. You name it, he'd researched it. Including some clearly forged charities and fabricated organizations. All of which were quickly disqualified.

Watching the games unfold, he'd realized that people were often paired up to help them overcome personal issues or to repair broken relationships. Until just now, he hadn't realized Maddie noticed the personal aspects of the groupings.

It was a pleasure to watch the contestants overcome fears and come together as a true team. Some fell in love, others built solid new relationships or reforged old ones.

The room hummed with conversation. Occasional bursts of laughter broke through and made heads turn. Everyone fell silent when Jenny, best known as Mrs. Claus, who was clearly in charge of the train's operations, walked through the crowd and stood behind the podium. Her gold-rimmed glasses shone on the bright light streaming through the windows. She had traded her usual white ruffled granny cap for a Santa hat.

"Good morning, everyone. I'd like to congratulate all of yesterday's teams. Particularly John and Mary, Team Paira-Parkas for their success yesterday. You went above and beyond and saved the Smith's Christmas." She paused and scanned the room with a huge smile. "It is December twenty-second. Today, our last two pairs will compete. Can I have Misty Simons and Thomas River step forward?" They stood, one on each side of the room. Jenny waved them forward.

"You will be known as Team Misty River." The crowd chuckled.

"Corny," Chris muttered. All the names had been. He wasn't sure why they were needed, but he appreciated the effort that went into naming each pair.

"Team Misty River, there are three hours until we arrive in Rapture Falls, which is a little-known town accessible only by ATV, four-wheel drive, or horseback." She smiled. "And by our wee train now that the rail line has been completed." The crowd cheered for the train's accomplishment.

"Now, Team Misty River, what you need to gather, is a two-sentence biography of every remaining contestant. The organizers of our amazing trip are creating a record of who is involved. Eventually, there will be a website for this year's trip, and if this trip is as successful at raising charity funds as it seems to be, for trips in the future."

She was drowned out by a wave of applause. "The catch is, we don't want normal bios. Not, Jenny

McCracken from Oakland, California. But something fun and unique about them. Challenge your fellow contestants to be unique."

"What if they sabotage us?" Misty asked.

"I cannot picture that happening. This contest has astounded me with the generosity, helpfulness, and general support you have shown each other. But if anyone is caught hampering your task, they will be disqualified." She answered a few more questions from Misty.

"Next up is Scott Bear and Becka Little. You'll be known as Team Little Bear." The crowd chuckled. Scott was an enormous man with a big fuzzy beard. He rather resembled a bear. When the crowd settled, Jenny continued. "There are two hundred twenty-five people on this train. Your goal is to collect one dollar from each of them and to get this guest book," she waved a small red and white book in the air, "autographed by each of them."

"What's the buck for?" someone asked.

"The money will be donated to the fund to bring a nurse practitioner to Rapture Falls."

"A buck doesn't seem like much," Chris mumbled, just as a voice down front said the same thing.

"True," Jenny agreed. "They are welcome to donate more, but each person must give at least one dollar. Twyla will accompany you to ensure you meet your task. You have until eight p.m. to finish." She made a few housekeeping remarks, and everyone set off.

"This should be interesting," Maddie said after the crowd cleared. "I get the distinct impression that Misty and Thomas have a history of some sort. And neither

Scott nor Becka seem comfortable talking to other people. They've pretty much kept to themselves."

"True. I've wondered why two clear introverts chose to compete." He wheeled himself toward a vacant table in anticipation of a filling breakfast. "I don't think I've seen either of them talk to more than a handful of people."

"I think it will be fun to watch them come out of their shells. They share the same charity, don't they?"

"Yup." He waved to a server who hurried over with menus, pulling at the hem of her elf costume and frowning. "It's a charity that helps children overcome their fears."

"I wonder what they are afraid of, besides other people?" she asked. "There must be a reason why they were both chosen.

Chris knew, based on their paperwork, but it didn't feel right to share the info with Maddie. Some things weren't other people's business. Scott had been badly bitten by a dog and had lived in terror for a decade before finding help. Becka was the victim of abuse at a relative's hand. Both had trouble forming new relationships with others. Their charity offered free counseling for troubled kids.

"How do you keep track of what they're up to when they're off the train?" she asked.

"I have a network of spies." He twirled his imaginary mustache like a villain from a black-and-white movie.

"Of course you do."

What she didn't know was that he'd been allotted funds for recruiting the assistants who were now on the train, either as paying customers or staff. He'd vetted all the staff, and it was no trouble to slip in the people he wanted working with him. Maddie didn't need to know that, because not knowing would allow her to interact with them more naturally. However, their benefactor had approved it.

She wasn't the only one with secrets. A niggle of guilt shamed him. He pushed it aside.

He wondered how the benefactor always seemed to be up on everything that happened and never seemed surprised when he checked in with his reports. Of course, with the digital tweaking of their voice during satellite calls, the person on the other end of the line could have been anyone. Likely some billionaire businessman.

Heck, for all he knew, they could be on the train.

Food for thought.

Speaking of food, he was famished.

They chatted briefly with the server before ordering. As she disappeared into the kitchen, Maddie looked at him. "Tell me you aren't going to miss all this intrigue."

"Of course, I am." He looked around. They were virtually alone in the dining car. One couple sat in the corner, too far away to hear their low voices. "I'm a private investigator. I enjoy snooping out people's secrets."

"But you're more than that."

He feigned confusion.

"You were in the army. You've done private security. I'm curious what else you've done."

She searched his face, and it was hard for him not to grin.

"Tell me about your other endeavors," she said.

"What was it you said earlier?" He paused and looked around the car, pretending to be thinking about what she'd said, though he easily recalled every word she'd ever said to him. His time with Maddie was burned into his brain.

Faking deep thought, he admired the Christmas decorations. Especially the gaily lit tree, all done up in silver and gold with multi-colored lights, so much like the ones from his childhood. "Oh, yeah. You said something about secrets being revealed in time. It'll all come out. Eventually."

"That is not fair." She crossed her arms over her chest.

He shrugged. "Where is that girl with my coffee?"

"Her name is Navia."

"I knew that, it just slipped my mind." He slid further into his old-man role. He'd investigated everyone involved.

He'd tried investigating Madeline Hayes and had come up with nothing. Absolutely nothing. He mentioned it to the benefactor on several occasions and was told to let it drop. They had personally vetted Maddie. One email had gone so far as to suggest that if he didn't drop it, he'd be replaced. Of course, that was long before the train left Denver. Now it was too late to fire him.

"Tell me something about yourself," he said. "Something I don't know." *Which was almost everything.*

She blinked twice and shifted in her seat. "I'm an only child."

"Are your parents alive?" Having gotten one answer, he pushed for another.

"No. Nor are my grandparents on either side. And I don't want to talk about them." Her frown deepened. "Want to go to see the carolers?"

"There are carolers?" He replied, knowing he wouldn't get any more answers about her personal life.

"In the central observation car at ten. We have just enough time to eat and get there. I love Christmas music, and I hear they have the best costumes. They're so realistic they could be in a Dickensian story. Some of them are in the group that performed when we made stops."

"I suppose we could go." He feigned reluctance. He'd go anywhere to spend more time with her. Yes, he was angry about her deception, but he understood her reasoning, which made him inclined to give her a second chance. Eventually, he'd like to be with her without his costume. Somewhere where he could be himself, without their secrets between them.

"If you don't think you'll be overtired," she said with a subtle nod at something behind him.

"I'm not that old," he grouched. "I can handle some Christmas carols."

"Oh. Can we go with you?" Dalton and Tess of Team Yip walked from behind him to the end of the table. Tess carried Dalton's small dog.

"Of course." He waved in a sit-down motion. "Join us here, and at the singing. If you don't mind a bitter old man's company."

The pair took seats opposite each other. Dalton surreptitiously wiped some crumbs off the table and checked the water glass for spots. Tess squinted at him, and he dropped his hands to his lap. While he was better, he still wasn't completely free of his over-fastidiousness.

Tess patted Chris's hand. "You aren't old, Mr. Watson."

"Call me Chris."

"Chris it is. I'm excited for the carolers. I wonder how they found them."

"I heard that some of them are staff," Maddie said. "Bruce, the bartender, mentioned it. I guess that means the rest are paying customers or contestants." She sipped her coffee and smoothed the white tablecloth.

Interesting. She was nervous. What else did she know that he didn't? And why hadn't he heard anything about the carolers performing today? He was well aware of their off-train performances. He must be slipping up. Probably because being with Maddie was so distracting. Distracting enough that he'd occasionally forgotten to use his old man's voice.

Breakfast turned into a rowdy affair with visits from ten different contestant pairs. Everyone recognized him and stopped to chat. One woman had a medical question for Maddie which she handled reluctantly, but with ease, and only after suggesting that they consult a doctor about it as it wasn't urgent. She had a wonderful bedside, or in this case tableside, manner.

Her reluctance to answer tweaked something in his mind. He had no idea where she went to nursing school. What kind of training or specialty did she have? Another deception? Or part of the same one? Because of yesterday's lie, doubts about her honesty were creeping in. The whole thing was, as his teenage niece would say, totally sus.

Katie O'Connor

# Chapter Three

The central observation car was packed. So much so that they could not get seats for the show. Disappointed, Maddie, Chris, and several others headed into the next car to wait their turn.

Jenny and one chambermaid, who must be doing double duty, started assigning times to come see the show. Maddie's group was scheduled for the next concert in forty minutes. Everyone crowded into Paige Chamberlain's tiny room to wait. She and her partner, Davyn Kayne, had completed their challenge to write and perform an original Christmas poem.

"They should have planned this better," Dalton grumbled.

Maddie smiled at him. Dalton was a stickler for organization. He was a lot like her father, who got upset when life wasn't perfect. Only Dalton was calm. Her father had gone into rages.

"Oh, don't fret about it," Tess advised. "Things happen. I'm sure they'll do better next time."

"Trust me when I say that it's impossible to predict how many people will show up at an event," Davyn said wryly. "I've had poetry readings where it was standing room only, and the next was attended by a whopping thirty people. And that was before I was accused of plagiarism."

"Have you forgotten?" Paige said, squeezing his hand. "You were exonerated and now publishers are clamoring for your work."

"Only because you are my muse."

Maddie sighed at the romantic comment. She adored couples in love. She snuck a glance at Chris, who was deep in conversation with John and Mary of team Paira-Parkas.

His eyes sparkled as he laughed over something Mary said. It took everything Maddie had to maintain her seat on Paige's bed and not go to his side. She was in so deep that she wanted to spend every second with him. He glanced her way and winked in direct opposition to his earlier anger. Heat flooded her cheeks. How could one man have such a devastating effect on her with a casual action?

*Probably because you have known no love in your life. Not since your grandmother and her dog died when you were twelve. Honestly, it's a wonder your parents even let you visit Nanna at all.*

She tried not to dwell in the frigid depths of her lonely past. But she was savvy enough to realize that her past left her vulnerable to the actions of others. It would be easy to fall for someone who was faking feelings for her, or who was trying to take advantage of her.

Not that she thought Chris was doing that.

Ironically, she'd had him, an investigator, thoroughly vetted by three different P.I. firms. Two from the U.S. and one from Canada where he resided, though not from his home province of Alberta. She'd been burned by a man once before and she wasn't letting anyone get close to her inheritance without knowing everything about them first.

Letting her romantic mind run free, she idly wondered where they would live if they became a couple. She'd taken the trust fund she received from Nanna and moved to New York City at eighteen when she left her family mansion. Her tiny apartment was more than enough to meet her needs, but way too small for two people. They'd need to find a new place. Somewhere where she could continue nursing.

Unskilled in anything at eighteen, she drifted from job to unskilled job until her parents passed away. Only then, after much soul searching, did she discover her passion. Helping people. Nursing school became her saving grace and changed the entire course of her life. Since the start of the research for this contest, a question plagued her. Where would she live after this was over? She was tired of New York's hustle and bustle. She wanted a simpler life.

A simpler life and a serious relationship headed for marriage. Maybe with Chris, if he was amenable, or if they fell into something more than friendship. Now was not the time to pursue a relationship. After the contest was soon enough. She had enough on her plate as it was. Later. Love could come later.

They'd known each other for a year, and she was still waiting for him to show his interest. If he didn't step up soon, she'd have to step outside her comfort zone and take the first step. She suppressed a wince. She'd been trained since childhood that she only needed her family. Not that they'd been the loving type. Nanna had taught her that love was important and worth having. The two ideologies clashed in her brain and her stomach with nauseating consequences.

Someday, she'd find the man she was learning she deserved. One who loved her for herself, not for her money. Her heart whispered that maybe that would be Chris.

*Maddie, stop fantasizing.* Her brain chided. *He's not for you, he's a simple man with simple tastes. He'll freak out when he finds out how much money you have, and that you're not just a nurse, you're a trust-fund baby. Your lies will drive him away. Forever. He won't understand your past and where it has led you.*

Shoving aside the depressing thoughts, she focused her attention back on the room where Chris was busy making horrible Christmas dad jokes. They were so groan-worthy that she had to join in the laughter. This was friendship on a level she was unfamiliar with. She'd never fit in at boarding school and her parents had refused to let her associate with local children. Now, she was loving every second of freedom and making new friends. She'd started expanding her circle in nursing school. On this train, in a matter of weeks, she'd built over a dozen friendships, which were more than she'd had her entire life.

It seemed like no time at all that they were seated at the edge of the central observation car, beside Tracy and Rex, waiting for the performance to begin. The room buzzed with cheerful chatter. About fifty percent of the crowd was from the contest. The rest were paying customers of the train's inaugural trip. She hoped this was the first trip of many. It had better be, since almost the entire route of rails had been laid for this trip. The Rocky Mountain Christmas train would ride again next year, and with luck, would have non-Christmas tourist trains running year-round. Otherwise, the expense would be all for naught.

She pushed the worry away. That was a thought for another day. She grinned at herself. She felt rather like

Scarlett in *Gone with the Wind* who'd kept pushing problems off to be dealt with later.

Chris reached over the side of his wheelchair and squeezed her hand. She glanced around to ensure nobody noticed. It would be terrible if anyone thought something was going on between them.

"What?" she asked, careful to keep her voice from disturbing the others.

"I just felt like it," he whispered. "I'm glad to be here with you. Christmas feels special this year."

"I agree."

"On which part?" He winked.

Until the last two days, he'd been strictly business. Now that he'd started winking, it almost felt as if he were flirting. But why would he flirt with her? She wasn't anything special, simply hiding her background as a nurse while pretending to be Chris's nurse. She almost groaned at the mental gymnastics that the thought had taken.

First, she fantasized about him, then she didn't feel worthy. She needed to banish the negative self-doubts her family had given her. She was better than that.

Chris nudged her with his elbow, and she realized she hadn't answered his question.

"Both, I guess. It does feel special, and I'm enjoying my time with you."

"I'd like to take you to dinner at the next stop."

The statement had her as giddy as a kid on Christmas morning. She banked her excitement. "We should wait until the journey is over."

"Do you want to wait?" He kept his voice low, but his face showed displeasure.

She giggled. "Not really. But how?"

"Let me arrange that. I'll let you know the plan."

She smiled her acquiescence and leaned back as the choir stepped in front of the crowd.

*Rocky Mountain Christmas Train*

Chris tapped his toes to the choir's singing. Their outfits were period-perfect, and he was happy to see some of his spies participating. He chuckled to himself. Being a private investigator was always interesting. While he primarily worked for corporations, he had other clients. He avoided chasing cheating spouses at all costs. He did a lot of work searching for missing people. Adoptions were a specialty for him.

This job for the Rocky Mountain Christmas Train had been a gold mine for his business. Most of the work had been straightforward, but there had been some unexpected twists and turns and more than a few scam attempts.

The biggest perk was spending the last year working with his nurse. Maddie was a woman unlike any he'd ever met. Sophisticated but down to earth. She seemed to have a modest background, though he hadn't confirmed that, but her clothing was top quality. They shared a sense of humor and enjoyed the same movies. While he hated detective books, she loved them. He had a secret passion for romance novels, particularly rom-coms. Not that he'd shared that with her. Especially since she claimed she rarely read them. Though he could easily picture them snuggled up before a fire reading romances to each other.

Cliff and Jenny joined the carolers as they sang *Last Christmas*. He chuckled.

"What are you laughing at?" Maddie asked between songs.

"Haven't you heard of Whamageddon?" He'd have sworn the whole world knew about it.

"What's that?"

"The goal is to avoid hearing Wham's *Last Christmas* for as long as you can. My receptionist and I have a contest every year. We bet fifty dollars that the other will hear it first. We donate the money to The Salvation Army Santa, who stands outside our building every year. It's all good fun and, truthfully, I like the song."

"I guess we lose together." She grinned at him. "Next year I'll beat you."

He liked the idea of a future with her. His biggest worry was that they didn't know each other well enough. Sure, they'd spent a year together on the investigations. They'd go through the information his team had curated and look for potential problems with candidates. Maddie was particularly adept at finding mistruths. She also focused more on their personal lives than he did. She spent days scrolling through social media. What she found often astounded him. Relationship problems, work trouble. Family illness. Why would people post that stuff? He never understood airing your dirty laundry in public.

While working together, they had shared a couple dozen lunches, maybe more. Part of him said to trust who she seemed to be...a nurse working for someone with a lot of money and a big heart. The rest of him was worried about not being able to find her on social media, or even her birth records. How had she hooked up with the organizer of this train? So many unanswered questions. Too many.

He'd let it ride for the moment. After this trip was over, he intended to press for answers. For now, he'd try not to think about it. He turned his attention back to the carolers who were singing *We Three Kings* with harmony that would have made a professional choir proud. Another two songs and they wrapped up the half-hour performance.

"That was beautiful." Maddie sighed. "I love Christmas music. I start playing it in October. It used to drive my family crazy." She frowned, as if thinking about her family annoyed her.

"October seems early. Mid-November, maybe." All around them, people stood and headed out the door on a wave of voices and a whisper of rustling clothing. "Shall we go get coffee?"

"I don't see why not. You need to keep your eyes and ears open, and you need to check on today's contestants." She looked around the room. They were alone. "Let me fix your beard. It's come loose." She pulled some spirit gum from her purse and dabbed a bit onto his cheek.

He inhaled deeply. Her touch was soft and brief, but it incited a masculine reaction through his entire body. "Thanks," he whispered, his voice gruff.

"Are you okay?"

He cleared his throat. "Just emotional about the music," he grumbled in his old man's voice.

"Christmas music makes me happy," Chantal said.

"Where did you come from?" Maddie blurted, her face pinkening.

Chris hadn't heard the telltale click of her crutches.

Chantal giggled. "The hallway. Mom says we're going to have tea and snacks. Do you want to come too? Mr. Chris and I can play cards." Her voice lilted with hope.

Chris chuckled. "Think you can beat me?" Chantal's laugh lifted his spirits.

"Yes. I beat you lots."

"Hm. Let's see, I've won thirty games, and you've won thirty-five. That's pretty close."

"I beat you five times more," she said proudly. "I can do math."

"You sure can. Lead the way." He turned and smiled at Maddie "Miss Maddie, shall we?"

"Whatever you wish, boss."

He did a double-take. It almost sounded like she meant something else. His mind flashed back over their year of knowing each other. She only called him boss when she was upset with him. Yet, right now, she was smiling.

Women! They were entirely too confusing, and she had him unbalanced.

They ended up at a table for four. Maddie, Chris, Chantal, and Joy. Seth was sitting across the room chatting with two of the contestants who had failed to meet their challenge through no fault of their own.

He waited patiently for Chantal to shuffle and deal a game cheekily known as Dummy Rummy. A simple game of collecting sets and runs in a particular pattern. It was a perfect game for kids and adults. Not too simple to bore the adults, not too complex as to confuse an eight-year-old.

They were into their fourth deal when Chantal looked at Chris. "Mr. Chris, did you used to be married?"

"Chantal, you can't ask a question like that. Mind your manners," Joy chided.

"It's okay," Chris muttered as he fumbled for an answer. It wasn't a question he'd expected to be asked, and he had no canned response. He went with the truth. "Once a long time ago."

"Is your wife dead?"

"Oh, gracious, no." He looked her straight in the eye. "Do you know how some people can be friends but not be married?"

"Like my mom and dad. Dad didn't like me, so he went away."

"I'm sure that's not true. You're a lovely girl. Sometimes people aren't made to live with other people. Or they aren't strong enough to handle trouble. My wife was like that. She was a special person, but I wasn't the right man for her. She went away and found a man who made her happier than I did. That's okay because I loved her enough that I wanted the best for her. Maybe your daddy left because he wanted the best for you." *Heaven save me from this conversation. And forgive me for lying to a child. He did not love his ex. Not even a bit.*

"Oh! Like Seth. I like Seth. Mommy does too." She reached out and patted Chris's hand. "Maybe you'll find someone nice to love. Like Mommy did."

"You're a very smart young lady, Chantal. I sure hope you're right." He glanced at Maddie. She looked as stunned as he felt. "Maybe somebody like Miss Maddie, but closer to my age." It was a direct message to his attractive nurse and judging by the smile blooming in her eyes, she'd caught his less than subtle hint.

Katie O'Connor

## Chapter Four

After dropping Chris off, Maddie stepped into her room and closed the door. "Whew," she whispered. What in the world was that? Chris had been flirting like a man on a mission. A mission to seduce her out of her better judgment. Wasn't it enough that they had a date, of some sort, tomorrow night in Rapture Falls?

"What are you going to do, Maddie?" She kicked off her shoes and paced up and down her large suite. There was no comfort in the lovely decorations or the gaily lit Christmas tree. Now that it was clear that they were headed for a relationship, it was time to tell Chris the truth. All of it. Every word. From her horrid upbringing to her multiple inheritances. From her lonely existence to the truth about their benefactor. Ya, that one was going to hit him like a cannonball.

"You should tell him now. Before it goes any further." She puffed out some rapid, nervous breaths. She couldn't. If she told him now, it would ruin any chance in the future. But if she waited, they might develop a relationship strong enough to stand the truth.

She wracked her brain for an escape route.

Over the past year, while working together, she'd spent most of her time in Edmonton so Chris could work for the train without giving up his entire practice. He had a nice slate of regular corporations who hired him. It made sense that he keep them happy, so they'd be around in the future.

She'd rented a furnished apartment only blocks from his office. She had loved summer in Alberta. The warm days and cool nights. Working together almost every day, they often went to a park for a picnic lunch. Taking their lunches or buying them from food trucks and street vendors. Her favorite had been the chili-cheese dogs with tons of mustard, mayo, and extra cheese. Hold the onion. Chris had loved the smokies, and she loved every moment with him. She'd started falling for him right away. Only knowing she had a job to do, that the success of the train's inaugural journey depended on them, kept her on track.

Winter was less accommodating, but on warm days, they'd visited the same vendors and taken their food back to the office. Sometimes she paid, others he did and put it on his expense account for the train. All the while, she fell deeper in love. And he didn't show a single sign of being attracted to her. The man was professional to the extreme. He carried himself with dignity and confidence without being unapproachable.

Oftentimes, she'd had to remind herself that he wasn't a rich entrepreneur with buckets of money. He had a healthy business, and he worked hard, but he wasn't wealthy. Still, he acted as though he did. Not in a bragging, look-at-me way. But in an I'm successful and you'd be smart to hire me way.

One blustery April day, near the start of their research, they'd bumped into a woman on one of their trips to grab lunch.

"Chris. It's so lovely to see you." An elegant blonde approached with wide open arms for a hug.

"June," Chris answered, ice in his voice and distaste in his eyes. He stepped back and after a long pause, the woman dropped her arms. "Where's Greg these days?" Chris asked with an uncharacteristic sneer.

June laughed lightly and the false joy grated on Maddie's nerves even as she wondered who the woman was and why there was such tension between her and Chris. After a short, stilted conversation, June moved on.

"Thank heaven that's done with," Chris exclaimed, glaring at June's back. "If I ever see her again, it'll be too soon."

"Who is she? If you don't mind me asking."

"Nobody of importance." He pasted on a fake smile. "Just a woman I dated once."

He'd refused to discuss June, though Maddie had brought her up a few times over the next months. Even now, she wondered if he'd meant that he'd dated June once. Or, if he'd meant that he'd dated her once upon a time, as in...had a serious relationship with her. And who the heck was Greg?

Now, after Chantal's innocent question, she was wondering about June once more.

A lightbulb clicked on in her head. "Well, I'll be robbed and left penniless!" Maddie paused in her restless pacing. June had to be the woman who Chris talked about while playing cards, and Maddie would bet her favorite designer bag that Greg was the man she'd left Chris for. "Holy crashing stock market!"

June wasn't just some woman. June was Chris's ex-wife.

Dang it, she felt like an idiot. She'd known he was married and divorced. And that his business partner had broken their agreement. Chris had had to start his company over. Why hadn't it dawned on her that June was his ex?

She grunted in disgust. Her dad, who had never hesitated to criticize, had been right. Sometimes she did have her head in the clouds and was oblivious to what was going on around her.

Now, it was all she could do not to knock on Chris's door and ask him. The only thing stopping her was that if she asked for his secrets, he'd ask hers and she wasn't ready to open herself up all the way.

She only had this afternoon, their date tomorrow night in Rapture Falls, and part of a travel day tomorrow to solidify her relationship with Chris. She wasn't risking that by sticking her nose into his past. It was enough to know that he'd been hurt, and that June was probably a liar.

They were spending Christmas Eve, Christmas Day, and Boxing Day in Rocky Mountain House at a private lodge. A short vacation gift that came with their jobs on the train. After that, they'd head home. She'd open up to him at the lodge. If this whole thing didn't blow up in her face before then.

She sat down and jumped back up again. She paced for a moment and forced herself to lie down on the bed. After failing to get comfortable, she got up and went to her computer. There were emails to check. If there was service. There were a few points along the route where service was sketchy, particularly if it was overcast or snowing.

Outside, the sky was bright and clear as the mountains swept past her windows. A beautiful day. Her email connected surprisingly well. She shot off a few quick replies and dug in her suitcase for her satellite phone to confirm tomorrow's arrangements. One of her many tasks on this trip was keeping ahead of the train and having the events all prepped. There was a paid contractor at every stop who coordinated local events.

Rapture Falls was tiny. Only five hundred residents. It was unlikely that there would be much media coverage, as there were no hotels and only one B&B. The contest's own media crew of three reporters had been covering on-train events and the events at stops. Their reports, blog posts, and updates kept up interest while they were between towns.

Putting away her computer and phone, she knocked on Chris's door. She and Chris needed to be out there, watching what was going on. "You ready?"

He opened the door. His face glistened.

"Did you just shave?" Heaven help her. He was gorgeous.

"I did. My stubble was snagging on the fake beard. Every pull and snag made my eyes water. Can't have people think I'm a weepy old man."

"As long as they think you're old. Beard up."

"Can you do it for me? It's a pain in the backside to get straight. I don't understand how I can shave in the mirror without issue but putting this thing on challenges my spatial awareness." He waved the beard around like a rag.

"Sure. If you sit, I'll be able to reach better."

He sat in the desk chair and tilted his face up. She dabbed glue on the beard and smoothed it over his face. Her fingers brushed his soft cheeks. Her heart went pit-a-pat and jumped around like she'd run half a block. She'd love to touch him every day.

Though her nerves were fluttering like butterfly wings, she could barely wait for their upcoming date.

## Chapter Five

Chris smoothed his collar and looked in the mirror. A knock sounded on his door. After a quick peek through the keyhole, he opened it.

Bruce stepped inside, shut the door, and looked around. "Nicer than I expected."

"It is a suite. One of the best on the train."

"You scored big. I'm in crew quarters. I share my space with three other guys. It's not bad, but it is crowded. The scenery outside makes up for it. Thanks for helping me get the job."

"No problem at all. You have the perfect outgoing personality to work with people. Besides, I needed a few extra eyes and ears, or I'd never pull off everything I had to do. And it's nice to spend time with someone, besides Maddie, who doesn't think I'm a crippled old man. This gig is getting old. Thanks for helping out."

Bruce was a friend's son and was aware that Chris wasn't all he seemed to be.

"If I didn't help out, Pops would kick my backside." He laughed. Abruptly, he sobered. "You floored me when you told me about you and Maddie. So, this date? Is it serious?" He sat in the desk chair and spun it around twice.

"Frankly, I'm not sure. She's an exceptional woman. Great person and all that. But she's got secrets even I couldn't uncover."

"Wow. Dad says you're the best. If you can't find it, nobody can. What does the benefactor say about it?"

He snorted. "That Maddie was fully vetted and to leave it alone. I've never actually spoken to the benefactor in person. Only by phone and the voice changes every time. They're using some kind of modulator and an untraceable number. I have no idea if it is a man or woman, or a group."

"So, they could be on the train?"

Bruce was quick on the uptake, that's for sure. "They could be. Not as a contestant. I vetted all of them. Maybe as a passenger. If so, they'd have to have gotten on at the start and still be here, wouldn't they?"

"Dude, you're asking the wrong man. I just work here." He tapped his fingers on the desk. "I love being your wingman and making sure it's safe for you to sneak out."

"I need to be careful. Too many contestants know this is my room. Or rather, they would if they were observant. If a younger man came out of an old man's room, people might start to wonder. I need you to make sure the coast is clear. Now, and later when we come back to the train."

Bruce rubbed his hands together. "I love the intrigue."

"Not so much intrigue as caution." He slipped into his suit jacket. "Do I look okay?"

"That is such a girl question." He pursed his lips and wrinkled his nose. "You'll do."

Chris shook his head. "Why did I even ask?"

"Did you guys date before this all started?"

"No actual dates, but we've had a dozen working dinners. We've had a few more during the trip. After we made our appearance at official events, we went to dinner. But always in costume, except in Boulder."

That had been a three-hour stop. They'd watched the contestants depart for their assigned tasks and headed out to pick up a few things at the mall and get some lunch. The food on the train was amazing. But sometimes a man wanted a wider variety to choose from. Or to eat without being watched. Perhaps it was because he spent his entire life watching people, but occasionally, being on the train felt a bit like he imagined a fish in a bowl would feel, and he could use a break from that.

Maddie had a few things she needed to pick up for herself, and he'd tagged along to the mall. He wasn't a shopper, but the time with her as she quickly made decisions without lingering or dithering had been pleasant and a nice insight into her personality. They were still there when a prank put the lights out. He was thoroughly annoyed when he learned someone had pulled the alarm in some kind of stunt.

They hurried out of the mall. Their ride wasn't due for two hours, but there was little point in staying in a mall without power. Luckily, they'd been on the ground floor. They headed to a steak and pasta restaurant across the street.

Chris, who wasn't in costume, held the door open for Maddie as fire trucks streamed into the mall parking lot. "After you."

"Thanks." They paused inside to allow their eyes to adjust to the subdued lighting. It was brilliantly sunny outside, and the small piles of snow on the sidewalks created a glare.

He blinked rapidly. "I can see how snow blindness happens." He waited for her to move inside and followed. It was well before the lunch rush, and they were seated right away.

"I wonder what made the lights go out." She flipped open her menu.

"I have no idea. I'm just glad we made it out and that you finished picking up what you needed." He opened his mend. "I saw a few people from the train. That couple with the matching outfits. Chantal and her mom were there with Seth. They must have been successful in the first part of their task."

"Oh, I hope they got out okay. I'm rooting for them."

"As staff, we're supposed to be unbiased," he reminded her as he turned to the lunch section of his menu.

"I don't care." She chuckled. "They're such a good pairing. I noticed yesterday that he was very uneasy around the child. It'll be interesting to watch their relationship develop."

"If it doesn't bomb."

"I've noticed that you tend to see the downside." She looked him right in the eye.

Discomfited, he looked away and said, "I think being negative, and maybe distrustful, is a natural side effect of what I do. There is a lot of mistrust and negativity in the investigation business."

"I suppose so," she replied slowly. "But you must find positives sometimes." Their server brought ice water and left them alone again. "I used to be extremely negative. A mindset I learned at my father's knee. Mother wasn't much better. I've worked hard to shift to positivity."

"You call her mother?"

"We weren't a warm fuzzy family. Physical displays of affection were frowned upon. Verbal affection never happened." She shrugged as if it didn't matter, but the hurt in her voice betrayed the truth.

"That's horrible. I'm sorry you went through that."

"Thanks." She seemed to be avoiding his eyes as she wrapped her arms around herself.

"My family is incredibly open with affection. Sometimes too much so. But I think I'd prefer that to what you suffered through."

"I'll let you know when I've experienced it." Her tone was light but wistful.

He reached out and patted her hand. "You deserve affection, Maddie. A lot of it. I've watched you this year. You're kind, and giving, and caring. You deserve those gifts in return." And he'd love to give them to her, but not until after their work contracts were finished. Her blush was adorable.

She was an intriguing combination of world-weary, sophisticated, and innocent. The more time he spent with her, the more fascinated he became.

"Let's not talk about me. Let's talk about you."

"What do you want to know?"

She answered without hesitation. "Why a P.I.?"

"I did a stint in the military because I wanted to serve my country. Luckily, while I did some peacekeeping, I never saw combat. What I saw were lies and deception everywhere I looked. Not so much within the army ranks, but in the countries I served in. The wife of one of my closest army buddies cheated on him. He was destroyed and he left the service. I served four years before I opted out."

"How did that lead to investigations?"

He laughed wryly. "That same buddy had a new girlfriend and wanted to be certain she was on the up and up. He asked me to follow her. One thing led to another, and I ended up taking a criminology degree with the end goal of opening my firm. For the most part, I've been successful." He refrained from mentioning the affair between his fiancée and his partner and how it ruined his life and his business. There was no need to sully this lovely lunch with the ugly details of the past.

He turned the tables on her. "How did you end up in nursing?" *And how does a nurse afford top-quality clothing like yours?*

"I had done some volunteer work at a women's shelter in New York. I loved being able to help people." She sobered. "We had a woman go into labor and nearly lose her baby when the medics didn't come fast enough. I held her hand through the entire ordeal, wishing I knew enough to help her. It was then that I decided to go to school and become a nurse. I did so with the express purpose of helping other people."

"And now," he added, "here we are on a train helping people compete for charity." He squeezed her hand, and she turned hers up under his and squeezed back.

"Chris? You still with me?"

Bruce's Aussie accent jerked him out of the past. "What?"

"Where'd you go? You zoned out, mate."

"Into the past." He checked himself over. "I think I'm ready now. Let the dating begin."

Bruce got up and ambled to the door. He popped it open and looked both ways. "Okay, you're set. The hall is empty. Have fun tonight."

"I sure hope so. Wish me luck."
"Good luck, mate."

Katie O'Connor

## Chapter Six

Maddie walked the short distance to the only restaurant in Rapture Falls. If the Rocky Mountain Christmas Train turned into a regular route, Rapture would greatly benefit. They were eager to allow the train company to build close to town and stop there.

It was roughly five hundred yards from the tracks to the family-owned restaurant, which stood between the general store and an empty building that was destined to be the clinic once their fundraising was complete.

Her breath created wisps of fog in the chilly air. It was cold, but not too cold for such a short walk. With no streetlights, it was dark, save for the six buildings on Main Street with their outdoor lights on. They glowed golden in the evening air. Beyond them, a smattering of houses were lit with holiday lights and inflatable decorations.

She wondered why Chris had insisted on meeting her instead of traveling together. Sometimes he was strange. She vowed to ask him his reasoning.

Surprisingly, the restaurant was warm, welcoming, and remarkably busy. She'd been expecting historic or retro. What she found was wood-look vinyl planking, high-backed booths, and white linens. Elegant silver lighting and an enormous wood-burning fireplace gave the entire place a homey feel. Looking around, she realized that it was full of train passengers. People were lined up waiting for tables. She wondered what to do. Far in the back, a man stood and waved.

Chris!

Thank heaven.

She made her way between the tables and joined him.

"Hi."

"Hi yourself," he responded.

"I see you got a table." She unwrapped her scarf and hung it on the hook on the edge of the leather high-backed bench seat.

"I took the liberty of prebooking." He remained standing beside the table. Freshly shaved and wearing a charcoal gray suit he was handsome and very elegant. He'd look equally comfortable at a high society dinner and a casual wedding.

"When did you do that?"

He chuckled. "Honestly, before we departed Denver. I booked a table in every town we stopped at. I like variety. Let me help you with your coat."

She turned and slipped it off her shoulders. He caught it and hung it with her scarf. "Please have a seat. I ordered tea."

She slid into the booth. "Thanks for booking, and the tea."

"You do prefer it in the evening, and I know you won't break the rules and have wine."

She laughed. "Are you kidding? There are at least five staff members here besides us. Of course, they don't know you're from the train. I'm not sure how I'll explain meeting you..."

"Easy. I'm an old friend. They don't need to know anything else. Or you could just ignore the question as if it were beneath you." He filled her small china cup and saucer from the family-sized teapot.

She blinked. It hadn't occurred to her to let a question go unanswered. "I never thought of that. Thanks again for the tea." She pulled the cup toward her and cradled it in her hands. The warmth was wonderful, and a distraction from his mesmerizing eyes.

"You are very welcome." He paused. "Thanks for coming."

"I said I would." She didn't understand his gratitude. Her word was her bond. She said she'd be here. Why would he doubt that?

"True. I worried that you'd back out."

Holy smokes! He must be nervous too.

"Chris. You're a nice man. I'm very pleased to spend time with you both inside and outside of our assigned roles. I think we could be good friends." His easy smile slipped away, prompting her to ask, "What?"

"I thought we were friends already."

Her stomach churned. "Well. Um. That is..." She reached for the right words. She was wary of sounding either too eager or too distant. *Why couldn't life be easier?*

He waited without saying anything. The silence felt more respectful than pressure-filled. Finally, she said, "We are friends. I consider us good friends. I feel..." Again, she paused. "This feels like a date. An actual date. Time to get to know each other better and see if something could develop between us. Is that weird?" She stared at her tea.

"Oh, thank God!"

Her head whipped up.

He grinned.

"I was worried you thought this was a business dinner. I asked as a date, and I thought you accepted it as a date, and then I began to doubt my memory." He shook his head.

"I was worried that I assumed too much." She laughed.

They made their selections from the chalk menu on the wall. Maddie chose the roast pork dinner. Chris had the baked salmon. Neither felt inclined to test the liver and onions.

"You know," she said, "I've never been to a place which only had three selections. I can't believe that with three mains, there are eleven dessert selections."

"I expect they prepped for extra guests, knowing the train was stopping. And dessert is the most important meal of the day."

They'd argued more than once about desserts. He thought they were for every day, and she relegated them to special occasions. It was one of the many things they agreed to disagree on. Of course, he was a runner and weightlifter, and she was more of a slow yoga girl.

Several people from the train stopped by to say hi. Maddie introduced them to her friend, telling them his name was Vincent. When the tenth person came over as they finished their deep-dish apple pie, she'd had enough. "Want to take a walk or something?"

Chris looked startled. "It's winter."

"Brilliant observation Mr. Obvious. We can get a hot drink to go and wander around town. Plus," she paused dramatically, "There are supposed to be Northern Lights tonight and I've never seen them."

"You'll love them. I've seen them from Iceland, Russia, and Nunavut. Let me just grab the bill and we're out of here."

"I can pay for mine." She reached for the wallet in her jacket pocket.

"If it's all the same to you, I'd like to pay. I did invite you."

"You do know that it isn't the 1950s, right?"

"I do. But I'm a bit old-fashioned. When you invite me, you pay. Deal?" He lifted one brow.

"I'll be holding you to that."

"Oh? Good. That means we're having another date." His grin was unrepentant. He stood and held out her jacket. "I've noticed that people pay at the register by the dessert counter." He slipped into his cozy-looking wool jacket and buttoned it up.

Outside, it wasn't any warmer than when she arrived. Blessedly, it didn't seem to be any colder either. She pulled on the knit cap she had in her pocket but hadn't worn on the short walk over. She wrapped her scarf snugly around her neck and tucked her hands into her pockets. "Which way?"

"I walked around earlier. There are benches overlooking the valley down this way. We can sit and look at the sky."

She looked up into the night. Swirls of green and blue rolled together. "Oh! Look." She gasped. "It's incredible." Chris took her by the elbow and led her forward.

"Wait until you see it over the valley. The entire sky is open and alive."

She split her attention between the path and the sky as they hurried toward the edge of town. She sat on the bench and leaned back to take in the splendor spread before her. "So pretty."

"Yes, you are." Christ slid onto the bench and wrapped his arm around her shoulder. "The sky's okay too."

She nudged him with her elbow. "Thanks for this. It's a memory of a lifetime." In silence, they watched the sky dance. "I wonder what causes the lights?"

"Charged particles from the sun hitting the gasses in the atmosphere." He dropped the information casually, as if everyone knew that.

"Really? I had no idea."

"It's true. You'll see more after a solar storm or flare. Occasionally, there are enough particles that the lights are seen almost worldwide."

"I must make a mental note to research the aurora borealis," she said.

"Talking to yourself?"

"Yup. I remember better if I say it out loud. It's how I got through nursing. I read the texts aloud. Repeatedly. Hearing is remembering."

"That's interesting."

"Oh, look. Pink!" Giddiness flooded through her. And not just because of the lights. There was an amazing feeling of kinship sitting here with Chris. Her heart was excited and strangely at peace.

*Was this love?*

*Had she fallen all the way in over the past year?*

*Maybe that weird feeling was indigestion?*

She turned her thoughts inward to examine what she was feeling. She was no stranger to heartburn, and this wasn't it. This was new and wonderful.

"Ever think about leaving Alberta? Moving someplace else?" She asked the question as it popped into her overactive mind.

"Hm. Occasionally. But I love Edmonton. Plus, I inherited a ranch in central Alberta, near Red Deer. I'd hate to give that up. Though I rarely get the chance to visit. My cousin runs it for me."

He didn't ask why she brought up the subject, but she heard the question in his voice. "I'm thinking of leaving New York. But I don't know where I'd go. Maybe someplace less busy."

"Like Edmonton?"

She laughed. "Edmonton's okay. But it's one thing to live there for a year for the sake of this contest, and another thing entirely to up and move permanently."

"True. But would you? Would you give up everything and move?"

"Under the right circumstances? Yes."

"Cool."

There was a depth of emotion in the understated response.

They watched the lights until the cold started making her toes cramp. "I think I'm chilled right through."

"We should go back." He stood and offered his hand. Icy cold rushed through her when his warmth was removed from beside her. He'd been keeping her warm, and she hadn't realized it. His arm slipped around her waist, blocking the light breeze.

Slowly, they walked down the path toward town, commenting on the Christmas displays. "The lights are beautiful. Amazing how both a natural phenomenon and a man-made one can be so inspiring. I want to spread the joy of Christmas all around."

"You've given me a lot of joy."

Warmth surged through her. This might just be the happiest day of her life.

## Chapter Seven

Chris texted ahead and Bruce was waiting as they neared the train. Maddie headed for the observation car to get them cocoa and tea. When Bruce gave him the all-clear, Chris slipped unnoticed back into his room.

Shedding and putting away his outerwear, he quickly tidied up. He lit his tree and turned on some electric candles that were scattered around the room. He'd been surprised to see them when he boarded, but their bases were rubbery, and they'd held fast for the entire journey. It helped that this was the smoothest set of rails he'd ever had the privilege of riding on.

"I wish this trip wasn't nearly over," he grumbled to himself. "Hard to believe there is only one day left." Frustration that he hadn't made more progress in solidifying a relationship with Maddie pressed on his chest. "Get a date commitment. Tonight," he muttered. "Ensure you'll see her after the trip ends."

"Great idea. But how?" he argued with himself.

Maddie's door opened. Her voice mingled with another female's voice. After a moment she said, "Goodbye," and the door clicked shut. Something thumped and rustled. He stuck his head through the open doorway between their suites.

"Hi." She grinned at him.

"Who were you talking to?" he asked casually.

"Oh, Mary. She walked me back and held the tray while I opened the door."

"Tray?"

"Mary's sweet and thoughtful. I was trying to juggle two mugs, and she mentioned seeing a tray earlier. She cleared it off, and we loaded it with snacks."

"I could use a good snack." He rubbed his tummy.

"When are you not eating?" she teased, setting a tray on her table. She shed her outerwear, hanging everything neatly as he watched, memorizing every movement. From the careful way she set the tray down to the sweet way, she tucked her hair behind her ears before sitting.

"I'm a big guy. I work hard."

"Not on this train," she quipped.

"Actually. I do. Bodyweight training. I've got a whole routine, and I use that bar." He jabbed a thumb over his shoulder at the workout bar she'd seen him using. "Every day. Snow or shine."

"Like the postal service?" She set the tray on his desk. "I brought cocoa for you, tea for me, cookies, and Nanaimo bars. I've never heard of them, but they look good. Though I don't need a second dessert."

"Legend has it that they were invented in Nanaimo, British Columbia." He reached for one and took a bite. Heavenly chocolate, coconut, and nuts flooded his senses. He savored the bite before adding, "I've tasted a variation called London Fog Bars, and they are my favorite Christmas treat. Thank you." He bit off a small piece and closed his eyes to enjoy the treat.

"That must be some great dessert judging by the expression on your face."

"Mm hm. Delicious. Almost as good as s..." He snapped his mouth shut. He wasn't going there. For all that their relationship was changing and deepening, physical intimacy was something that had never come up in discussions. If she wasn't ready to go there, neither was he.

His eyes popped open at her laugh.

"If they're that good, I have to try them." She cleared a few things off her table, stacking them neatly on the end of her bed. She shifted everything from the tray to the table. "Come and sit with me."

The soft welcome in her voice slipped under his guard and into his heart, and he sat, sliding the last bite of his bar into his mouth.

She put a bar onto a napkin and sliced it with her fork. She eyed it warily, making him laugh. "You're sure these are good?"

"Rich as sin and decadent. Try it." He made an eating gesture.

She tilted her head. "Here goes nothing."

Her ecstatic moan shifted his mind to other, more earthly pleasures. *Holy secret identity Batman.* Her eyes fluttered shut. Never in his entire life had he seen someone give themselves so fully to a dessert. He banked his soaring libido and cleared his throat. "Well?"

"You're right." She smiled sweetly. "This is better than..." she paused dramatically. "Better than snow." Her smile morphed into a smirk.

"Tut tut. Ms. Hayes. You'll make a man think naughty thoughts."

"You started it." She licked her lips and took another bite.

He watched fascinated, as she ate the entire morsel. Sweet heaven, he was hooked. On her. Her absolute enjoyment of life. On everything about her. So much so that at that moment, he didn't care about not knowing who she really was.

"Have another square," he suggested. "You've only had one.

"And you've had three," she teased.

He had eaten three of the small confections she'd brought back. The Nanaimo bar, a date square, and something with colored mini marshmallows.

"I don't eat sweets often. They're my nemesis. If I eat one, I eat them all. You'll have to take those with you when you go." She picked a dessert to nibble.

"I can do that. Gladly. Tell me the best thing about your childhood." he asked, taking advantage of her obvious enjoyment of the treat.

She dropped the dessert back on the plate, rose and walked to the bed, and grabbed a throw off the end, beside the pile she'd set there earlier. She wrapped it around her shoulders and settled against the bed's headboard, her arms wrapped around her knees. "There's nothing to tell."

"Come on, Maddie. One good thing?"

"Fine," she snapped, her eyes shooting sparks. "My Nanna. She was the only bright spot in my life. Ever. Nanny and her dog, Brutus. Everything else was pure crap."

Her words landed like knife wounds to his heart. How badly had she been hurt to react so harshly? "I am so sorry that your life wasn't pleasant." He leaned forward and filled his voice with sympathy.

"But yours was." She sounded accusatory. Her eyes shut and her shoulders shook.

This was not going the way he intended. "Maddie? Look at me, please. I just want to get to know you better."

"Want to know me?" She snapped. "I grew up with parents who didn't give a crap that I was alive. I was there as the required progeny to take over the company. Love? Don't even ask. There was none. From three years old until I was twelve, I spent two weeks a year at Nanna's. One in the summer. One at Christmas while my parents toured whatever European city was the current rage."

He reeled back from the anger in her voice. "That's awful. Nobody should treat a child like that."

"I survived. But not well. When Nanna passed, she left me a small inheritance. The day I turned eighteen I took the money and moved out. Want to know why?" She didn't pause, not even for a breath. "Because I was turning into them. Becoming rude and demanding to our employees. Treating them like slaves. I had no friends because I wasn't allowed to associate with regular people. I wasn't allowed to do anything I wanted. There was an image to maintain. I hated every second of it and when I realized what, who, I was becoming I bolted."

He applauded. "Good for you. I'm proud that you decided to leave such a horrid place." Her eyes were moist when she looked up, but her mouth held the barest hint of a smile. "You left, and from everything I've witnessed about you, you've changed from that person. I've seen you interact with people. I've seen what's in your heart. You are a good person, Madeline Hayes. You really are."

"Thanks." She sniffed and grabbed a tissue to blow her nose.

His mind shifted gears. She must know the benefactor from school, or somehow because of her inheritance. How small is small? He let the thoughts slide, reassuring himself that she promised to tell him everything.

The train shifted. "Hey, we're moving."

Her smile grew wider. "Didn't you know? We're rolling tonight. We want to be in Rocky Mountain House early enough that people who choose to can make it to Calgary or Edmonton to catch flights home in time for Christmas."

"Right. I forgot about that." Was it any wonder it had slipped his mind? He was caught up in his role as a rich old man, in supervising the contest, and in getting to know Maddie. Life was coming on...well like a freight train.

"Maddie?"

"Yeah?"

He got up and got her a bottle of water from the tiny bar fridge. He passed it to her. "I'd like to spend some time with you. We're both staying at Hunter's Lodge for a few days. I'm booked until the new year. I'd like to see you, date you while we're there. See where this relationship goes when we don't have the pressures of work dragging us down."

"It drags you down?" Her brows clenched together. "It exhilarates me."

*That's what she's taking from my request? Not good.*

"Drags down isn't exactly the right terminology. You said it yourself...fraternizing isn't the wisest thing.

Once we hit Rocky, my only obligation is a final report. I'm sure yours is the same." She nodded, so he continued. "I meant we'll have more time to ourselves and no worry about being seen or outed by contestants. We'd be able to date like normal people. I love being with you, but I'm tired of being Old Man Watson. I want to be me."

"I'd like that." She twisted the cap off the bottle and took a drink. "Yes, Chris, I would like to date you and see where it goes." Though her eyes were still watery from her heartfelt emotional outburst, her smile was wide and welcoming.

This was the woman he was falling for.

"Want to watch a movie?" she asked.

Knowing that she was turning off the discussion, he agreed. They settled on a movie that was supposed to be

*Rocky Mountain*
*Christmas Train*

a comedy but ended up being more of a romance. The male character was hiding his identity as a member of a small European country's royal family. As the movie progressed, Maddie grew more and more fidgety, until he was tempted to ask her what was wrong.

Maddie shifted on her bed. Her shoulder brushed Chris's, and she shifted again. The temptation to lean into him was almost overpowering. He'd learned part of her past and hadn't blown a gasket. At least not yet. The main character in the movie lied for the seventeenth time, she was counting, and she winced.

*Did the stupid movie have to parallel her own life so closely?* Guilt clawed at her insides. Her lies burned in her stomach like acid. She wiggled again, but her conscience didn't clear. She picked up the remote and switched off the TV.

"What did you do that for? We're just getting to the best part."

"You've seen it before?" She pivoted to see his face better.

He shrugged. "Maybe."

"You watch rom-coms?"

"Um. Yes. I love a good romance. Especially one with twists and turns."

With luck, that feeling would carry through after her confession. The need to tell him her truth bubbled relentlessly.

"I know who the benefactor is," she blurted. She twisted her hands together in the blanket on her lap. She twisted and turned until it was a huge knot.

"I guessed that when you said you talked to them. How long have you known?" The question held a depth of accusation that wasn't revealed in the words, only in the tone.

"From the outset."

"So, all the time we worked together in Edmonton, you knew?" He jumped off the bed and stared down at her.

"Yes." She barely squeezed the word past the lump in her throat and her dry lips.

He glared. "Well?"

"Well, what?" She shook her head, pretending not to know what he wanted from her.

"Tell me who it is. It's late enough that it doesn't matter."

*Oh, but it did. Way more than he'd ever fathom.* She untangled her hands from the blanket and stood up. She wrapped it around her shoulder as she had earlier. There was no comfort in its soft warmth. The expression on his face went from wary to angry to expectant. Her windup alarm clock ticked off seconds like a bomb.

"I've known her a long time. Most of my life."

"I thought you didn't have friends. That's what you implied."

"I didn't."

His frown deepened, and he blinked. She could almost see the gears in his head turning. "Care to explain?"

She puffed out a breath and sipped her water. It landed in her stomach like a tsunami on a beach and threatened to ricochet back out. She swallowed it back down.

"Chris," she began, and faltered. She tried again. "I..." *Just tell him, before the deception kills you. Holy Christmas, she didn't want to confess but holding it in was making her physically sick. He'd hear the truth, then leave her. She wasn't ready for that. She loved him.*

His arms crossed over his chest.

She puffed out a long, slow breath that did nothing to calm her.

"Chris, I inherited money from Nanna." He made a weird, I know that face. "When my parents died, I inherited more. A lot more." She whispered an obscenely high number.

His mouth dropped open. "You did not just say—"

She cut him off. "I did."

He took two quick steps back and bumped into the door. He stared like she was a monster. He frowned. Sudden realization showed in his eyes. "You're the benefactor? Son of a..." He glared. "No wonder I couldn't find anything out about you. You've got money enough to hide anything. Who are you really?"

"My real name is Jennifer Madeline Astor-Hayes. My mother never took my father's last name and got saddled with a hyphenated one. I changed it when I left home at eighteen."

"As in Franklin Astor, the reclusive billionaire owner of eleven sports franchises and three U.S. banks?" His hands flailed around like he was trying to grab onto reality.

She nodded.

"And at no point in the last year did you trust me enough to come clean? To at least hint about who you were? Or that you were funding all of this?"

"It did. More times than I can count. Every single day. But I couldn't. I couldn't trust you at first."

"And later?" He barked out the question, his voice harsh and too loud.

"By the time I realized I was falling for you, I was in too deep, and it was too late." She shivered. She was freezing.

"Why now? If I can even trust your answer."

"I figured out about you and June. It's so much like my own story. Then, tonight, I realized how deeply I've fallen for you. Then the movie. It all added up."

He interrupted her. "How is my story with June like anything in your life?" Sarcasm rolled off the words.

"Because." She choked on the confession. "Before I went into nursing—"

"Are you even really a nurse?"

"Stop interrupting me!" she shouted. He mimed zipping his lips. "Before I went into nursing. I met a guy. He seemed nice. Really nice. Until he didn't. Turns out he was after the money. He knew someone who knew my father. He knew about the inheritance and tried to steal it from me. I caught on at the last second when the bank refused to give me a huge chunk of money, cash, without a waiting period. I didn't even know they could do that."

"They can't."

"The banker was Nanna's neighbor's son. I kept the money there when she passed. He was a lot smarter than I was. When my ex threw a tantrum over not getting the money fast enough, I clued in." She buried her face in her hands. "God, I was such an idiot."

"Lots of people get taken advantage of every day." He sounded understanding, which only made it worse.

"Not me. Not since then. I didn't want to take that risk with you. I didn't want to be wrong about what I felt. So, I lied."

"Even after you learned how I feel about the truth? After learning what June did to me? How could you?"

"I am so sorry, Chris. I never meant to hurt you." She stepped toward him. He held up his hands as if warding her off. She grabbed his arm. He pulled her hands off and stepped back.

"I can't believe...I need time to think." He stormed to the adjoining door and whirled around. "You should have told me. If not from the start, at least when you first confessed to knowing the benefactor." He laughed harshly. "Jokes on me, isn't it? You're the person funding this whole thing." He shook his head.

"Can we talk about it?"

He reared back. "No." He swung around into his room and closed the door behind him.

The soft click of the latch was like a gunshot. It echoed through the room and slammed into her heart. She clutched her chest and fell to the floor, weeping.

# Chapter Eight

During the night, after he left Maddie's room, the train stopped moving. The lack of motion woke him from a troubled sleep. Outside, not even the moon lit the darkness. The train's colorful Christmas lights were off, and it was cold. Chris rolled over in bed and clicked the light on the small bedside table. Nothing.

"Shoot."

Still train. No lights. Something was wrong. Very wrong. Being stuck in the middle of the Rocky Mountains on a private rail line in the middle of December was a recipe for disaster. He rose and dressed in street clothing, ignoring the old-man costumes virtually spilling out of his suitcases. Lucky for him, the train carried both contestants and paying passengers. He'd used his actual looks and voice several times. Right now, he was bundling up and heading out to see what he could do to assist the train staff. His military survival skills could come in handy.

He tapped lightly on Maddie's door. After last night, he might never speak to her again, but he had to be certain she was okay before he checked on anyone else. He lied to himself that he was checking because she was his boss. It sure wasn't because he cared.

The door opened.

She stood on the other side wrapped in her parka and scarf, her blonde hair a disaster. Holy smokes. Even red-eyed and sleep-deprived, she was gorgeous.

"Chris. I was just going to knock. Something's wrong. What do we do?"

"You stay here," he advised. "I'm going to see what I can do to help."

"Don't be ridiculous. There are children on this train. I'm coming. I can help." She stepped into his suite. "Let's go."

He banked a sigh. "Promise me you'll stay safe and keep warm."

"I'll be as warm as you." She shook her head the way she did when he exasperated her. "Let's go. It's cold."

"Fine." He opened his door. "Call me Vincent. That's the name I've been using when I'm not Chris."

"Where did you come up with that?" she whispered as they traipsed down the hall toward the central lounge car with its wood-burning stove.

"Grandfather's name." He suspected she already knew. Surely if she'd been as cautious as she claimed last night, she would have had him investigated.

People stepped out into the hall. "Keep going forward," he advised. "There should be heat further up. Some of the cars have wood stoves." Fortunately, the idea of being warm got everyone moving and prevented a bottleneck.

In the central car, number twenty-five of fifty, Bruce, the head bartender, was cheering everyone up with his jovial Aussie accent and telling groan-worthy dad jokes. "Hang tight, mates. There's water heating on the propane stove. We'll have hot bevies quicker than you can say tie me kangaroo down."

Chris and Maddie followed him into the small kitchen. "What other cars have heat?" Chris asked.

"All the kitchen and dining cars. The forward and rear observation cars." He sighed. "That's it."

"Okay," Maddie declared. "Vincent and I will herd everyone that way. We'll make sure nobody gets left in a suite alone. Where's Jenny?"

"Haven't seen 'er yet. I expect she's busy trying to contact the benefactor. Cell service sucks in this zone."

"Good to know."

"I'll head forward and knock on all the suites. Maddie, you go back. Bruce, I suggest you round up some staff to assist you. Isn't Paige from Team Rhyme and Dine a server? Maybe she could help. I'll send her this way."

After a moment of planning, they set out.

He pounded on every door and was greeted by anxious or angry faces. Before long, he was at the front of the train and nearly certain that everyone was headed toward warmth. He wondered how Maddie was making out. More importantly, was there anything she could accomplish that he couldn't? She was the brains behind the contest.

He made his way forward and cautiously climbed into the front engine.

The head conductor, Bob Siffeldeen, was slumped over at the controls, his face white. Cautiously, he leaned Bob back and took his pulse. Thready, but there.

"Shoot." He must have had a heart attack or a stroke. He made Bob as comfortable as he could. Thank heaven for mandatory first aid classes in the army. After shedding his jacket, Chris covered Bob with it. He shut the engine's door and hurried backward toward help.

He entered the first car after the engine, the forward observation car, and hollered, "Does anyone here know first aid?"

Everyone looked around, but nobody came forward.

He grabbed the first person he could reach. "Go find Maddie, the woman who nurses the old guy, whatever his name is. We need a nurse up front, in the engine car. Now!'

The man, John from Team Paira-Parkas, looked stunned but complied.

"Send anyone with first aid training," Chris called after him. "The train must have more than one trained person."

John waved to acknowledge he heard and disappeared through the back door of the car. His partner, Mary, stepped forward. "What can I do?"

"I need blankets. Lots of them and see if the kitchen has hot water bottles or those break-open hot packs."

"Okay." She reached into her pocket and pulled out a couple of pocket warmers. "I'm a cold wimp. I brought these." She thrust them into his hands. "Take these. I'll find more."

She turned and grabbed a lady sitting in the first chair. "You. Come with me. I need more hands." Fortunately, the woman who had been listening didn't hesitate. She jumped to her feet and took off.

Chris looked around until he found a burly man. "Keep everyone in this car, and when they get back with medical aid or blankets, help them to the engine. There's barely room for me, so don't let more than one person pass at a time."

"You've got it."

"And find me some aspirin."

"I have Tylenol," the man offered.

"It has to be aspirin."

A woman thrust a bottle into his hand. "Take this."

"Thanks." He hurried back to the engine. Bob was coming around a bit. His speech was slurred, but he showed no facial signs of stroke. That was a good thing. A heart attack was no picnic, but a stroke could be worse.

"Hang tight, Bob. I've got you." He fumbled some pills into his hand. "Take these. Chew them. They'll help."

Bob blinked but did as he was told, wincing at the bitter taste.

The door cracked open, and the burly man thrust a jacket at Chris. "Take this. It's freezing out there."

"Who's watching the door?"

"I've lined up some big guys to help out. We've got it handled. The server, the one with is helping us."

"Twyla."

"Right, that's it. I forgot." The man's face turned red. "My wife always complains about my inability to recall names."

Chris struggled into the jacket.

"I'm Darrod," the man said. "Take this." He thrust another jacket at Chris. "The car's warming up now that the stove's going full blast." He stepped back and closed the door.

Chris covered Bob's legs with the jacket, wrapping it around his legs and zipping it up. Where was Maddie?

Rocky Mountain
Christmas Train

Maddie went door to door, waking people and sending them towards warm cars. She had to make sure everyone was safe. Where in the world were the medical personnel? There should be two other nurses. The rest of the staff were busy organizing hot drinks and extra blankets for the people huddled in the heated cars.

"What happened to the heat?" she muttered as she made her way back to her suite. "And why are we stopped?" The hallway was deserted. The wind howled outside, and gusts of snow battered the windows, sounding like pellets.

She slipped into her room and dug into the suitcase tucked deep in the back of her small closet. She pulled out a satellite phone and flipped it on.

"Yes." The signal was weak, but it was there. She punched in a number from memory. It wasn't a number she ever planned to use, but she needed to line up help, and this was the best way to get it fast.

Her lawyer answered with a bite of anger in his voice. "Look, Bill. I don't have time for your complaints. This is important. The train has stopped. I don't know why. We may need emergency evacuation. It's minus forty. People are at risk."

"I told you this train trip was a stupid idea."

"Can it, Bill. This is serious. Say you'll help if we need it." Bill's continued complaints about the trip had been a sticking point between them. The man had been her father's lawyer. After their last argument, she had decided to replace him. She just hadn't had time yet. She prayed he'd come through today.

Bill's wife came on the line demanding to know what was going on. Maddie explained briefly.

"Go, dear. Do what needs doing. I'll organize the troops. We'll wait for your call."

"Thanks, Gina."

Gina was busy chastising Bill when Maddie hung up. Gina was dependable in a pinch and much less quick to anger than Bill. He was gruff and short-tempered, but he knew the people to get things done.

She grabbed a backpack and filled it with medical supplies. If the paid medical staff were too busy, she'd add her skills to the mix. She buried the phone in the bottom of the pack and headed back toward the front of the train.

The rear was cleared, at least of the people who answered their doors.

In the hallway, she ran into Jenny.

"Oh good. I hadn't seen you and was coming to check. We're using the master keys and cards to check all the rooms. Is Chris here?" Jenny looked around as if she expected Christ to pop out of the oak woodwork.

"Chris is up front. Or he was the last time I saw him."

"Where is he? I didn't see him anywhere. I've been in every car."

A chambermaid, bundled in a jacket and hat, came toward them, so she pulled Jenny into her cabin.

"I have to tell you something."

"What?" Jenny looked anxious to get back to work.

"You have to hear this." She sucked in a deep breath and coughed as the frigid air slammed into her lungs.

After a moment of coughing, she said, "Chris isn't who he appears to be."

"This isn't the time for true confessions."

"Look, Chris is a private investigator. He's up front, not in the wheelchair. He's a regular guy. He works for the benefactor."

"How do you know that?"

"That doesn't matter now. I've called for help. It's coming, but I don't know how soon it's arriving."

Jenny's eyes opened wide. "Holy Christmas cookies. You're the benefactor. Son of a Christmas elf."

"How did you figure...never mind. I don't have time to explain. We need to find out what happened. Continue as if you're in charge, which, for all intents and purposes, you are. I'll work in the background. Once we know what we're facing, I'll let the calvary know. Help is lined up and will be ready to go when we know exactly what we need."

"Does Chris know?"

"Yes." She blinked back tears. "He's mad."

"He should be. You lied to him." Jenny threw her arms around Maddie. "Girl, you are in so much trouble. And I have so many questions. We are so going to talk when this is over."

"I know." She stepped back. "You talked to Chris at the mall in Boulder. Tall man, dark hair. You saw us outside the cookie place."

"Holy smokes. I thought you met him there. I had no idea. He's hot." She stopped talking and blurted, "So hot. You sneaky devil you."

"Keep it to yourself if you see him and call him Vincent. The contestants think he's a paying passenger." She shoved Jenny toward the door. "You're in charge. I'm a nurse. Let's figure this out."

Together, they hurried forward. The first thing to figure out was why the train wasn't moving and why they had no lights. Meanwhile, they'd keep everyone calm and come up with a plan.

"Maddie! There you are." Twyla hurried up to her and grabbed her by the arm. "Vincent is in the engine. He would like to talk to you." She made a wide-eyed expression that managed to express urgency.

"Are you okay here?" Maddie asked Twyla.

"I'm good. We're good. I've got a couple of contestants helping serve hot drinks. Jenny, we need to talk." She shooed Maddie toward the front of the train as she pushed Jenny toward the bar area of the car.

The observation car was crowded with people huddled together on and under blankets. They leaned left and right out of the way as Maddie pushed toward the far door.

"I need to get to the engine." She stared up at two massive men blocking her path. She recognized them as passengers, not contestants.

"You Maddie?" The one on the left asked and pulled his Santa hat low over his ears.

"Yes. Chri-Vincent is looking for me." Whew, she'd nearly revealed Chris's identity. Not that it mattered at this point. With only hours left until Rocky Mountain House, if they got the train moving, it wouldn't hurt if people learned who he was.

"Step carefully. It's slippery now that the snow is coming in hard." He opened the door and accompanied her outside. "Climb down here." He climbed down a built-in ladder and turned to assist her. They shuffled through the snow, and he boosted her onto the deck of the engine.

"Why isn't it running?"

"No idea. Talk to them." He squeezed up behind her and opened the door.

"Maddie. Finally. I think Bob's had a stroke. Maybe a heart attack. He needs medical attention. I gave him a couple of aspirin."

"Step aside. I need room to examine him." Chris squeezed himself into a corner. He stood there, wincing. "What?"

"I've got a lever stabbing my butt. I'm good."

She pulled out the small medical bag from her pack and examined Bob. She asked him questions, and he nodded. He couldn't seem to form words without his teeth chattering.

"Good news, Bob," she said after a thorough exam. "I think it's your heart, not a stroke. But you need to be warmer and, as Chris says, you need medical care." Shoot, she'd used his name.

Bob looked back and forth between the two of them and frowned.

"Okay. Fine. His name is Chris. The old dude in the wheelchair. I'll explain later." She bundled him back up. "We're going to move you back to a car with a fire and warm you up. Who is your second in command?" She was in charge of the contest and the contest staff. While she owned the train and the line, she was smart enough to put the proper people in charge. The chef controlled the kitchens and wait staff. There was a head chambermaid. Bob controlled the engineers and maintenance staff. Everyone reported to Jenny, who reported via phone or email to Maddie.

Bob gestured weakly toward the floor. Maddie bent over and saw a built-in box. "Okay, once we get you out of here, I'll look. I'm assuming there's a list?" Bob nodded.

"Drink?" he whispered.

"We'll get you some ice chips." He grimaced. "Or sips of warm water. You can't drink a lot until we know what's going on."

He frowned.

She stuck her head outside and hollered over the wind to the large man still waiting there. "I need you and another guy to help Bob to the next car. Have someone help you and get someone to clear a space by the fire."

"Righto." He hurried away.

"Look," she said to Bob and Chris. "We're in a mess. We need to get the train going somehow. I'm not sure why we stopped. But we have to get going. Any ideas Bob."

He shook his head. "Big bang. Sputter. Stop. Panic. Chest hurt." He grunted out each of the words separately.

"Okay. Crap." She'd paid for a full inspection and upgrade on the train. There should be nothing wrong with it. *Note to self...three engines on the next run. If there was a next run. One wasn't enough to pull a train this big through the mountains. She should have planned for this.* "Okay. We'll get someone in to fix it. First, we need to get you out of here."

The door opened, and wind and pellets of snow blustered in. She hopped down, out of the way, and stood back while Chris and the two men gently hoisted Bob out and carried him to the next car.

She hurried after them, trusting Chris to return and close up the engine. Not that it mattered at this point. Still, there was hope that the secondary engineer could do something.

After being in the frozen engine and out in the wind, the observation car felt like heaven. She stepped inside and followed the men to the stove where Jenny stood with a passenger.

"Maddie, this is Melvin. He's an E.R. doctor."

"Melvin. Nice to meet you. This is Bob. I suspect a heart attack. I'll leave you to look after him. Have someone find me if you need anything. I'll locate another nurse and send her to you. She must be in one of the other heated cars."

Jenny thrust something into her hand. "Walkie-talkie. It's on channel ten. Keep it on."

"Where'd you get this?"

"A passenger had them to communicate with her kids. They got on a couple of stops ago. Melvin has one. I have the other. I'm taking one to the far end. At least we can keep in touch until the batteries die. I'll find that nurse. You and Vincent can figure out the plan."

Chris, who had been listening, scowled, but he followed them out of the car.

She huddled herself in the corner of the next car. Chris glowered at her.

"Look. I've phoned for help and now that I have a better idea about Bob, I have to call again. I'm not sure what we can do, but at least we're in an open area. They might be able to land a helicopter for Bob."

"And the rest of the passengers?"

"I'm working on it. I could use your support, not your anger. Save it for a better time." His frown made her wince. "Please."

"Is everyone accounted for?"

"I'm not sure. Okay, step one. We put one of the maids in charge of checking that all passengers and crew are someplace warm. We continue to check every suite using the master key to ensure nobody got missed." Panic rose in her throat. Somebody could freeze or be hurt. This was a nightmare. Unable to control herself, she twitched and shivered as fear threatened to overwhelm her.

Chris grabbed her by the shoulders and shook her lightly. "Get a grip. We've got this. We have contact outside of the train, right?" She nodded. "Good. We can organize here. It'll be daylight in a couple of hours, and if nothing else, we can haul everyone out with snowmobiles or dog sleds."

"A new engine. They could run a new engine out and hook up."

"Brilliant. Now you're thinking."

She dropped her pack on the floor and pulled out the phone. She hit redial. "Bill, we need an engine and an air ambulance. We've got a man down with a heart attack."

Christ held up his phone. She read off the GPS coordinates. Thank heaven they had signals! She listened for a minute and said, "No. We're good for now. It's blustery and snowing, but we've got limited heat until the wood and propane run out."

She clipped the enormous phone to her belt under her jacket.

"Can we talk about it?" She looked up at him.

"No."

"Come on, Chris. That's not fair." Not that she blamed him. He had every right to be mad at her. But nothing was solved by avoiding the topic.

"Maddie," he sighed. "I can't talk about it. Not now. I need time to work it out in my head. There's too much to do. People are in danger of freezing. Not immediately. But if the temperature drops, there could be serious problems. Your lies will wait. I'm going to help Jenny. Go look after Bob. Or something." He stormed away.

Steel bands tightened around her chest, and tears brimmed in her eyes.

No!

She would not cry. He was right, damn him. There wasn't time for tears or recriminations. She'd messed this up, and she'd solve it. She'd get them out of this disaster of a mess, and then she'd hunt Chris down and make things right. At the moment, she had no idea how, but she'd find a way. Blotting the tears with her sleeve, she dragged the phone back out.

She called her Rocky Mountain House contact and explained the situation. "There must be a snowmobile club or something there," she said. "Find them. Get some rides out here. We have little kids who need to be warm. I don't care what it costs. Buy them a clubhouse. Do whatever you need to do. Just get it done."

She winced. She sounded like her father. Shouting orders, buying her way out of trouble.

"Sorry. That was harsh. Do your best to get someone out here to start offloading passengers. At least the youngest and oldest. We can house them in the train station for the time being. Please arrange for additional hot food and drinks and let the hotels know that the guests may be delayed. Please ensure that everyone's room is held."

*I should build my own hotel.*

After ensuring everything would be handled, she returned to Bob and forced thoughts of Chris into the background as she unzipped her jacket to let the heat of the fire in.

"Hey, Bob. We've got an air ambulance coming. I'm just waiting on timing. It won't be long. We aren't far out of Rocky."

Bob smiled weakly. "Sixty miles."

"Good to know. I'm going to get that book and find your replacement."

"Sick."

Shoot. Crap on a cracker. Now what?

"Okay, who's in line after that?" He wrinkled his brow. "Never mind. I'll get the book and handle it. You rest. And know that you'll get the best medical care I can hire." The tension in his face immediately eased. Bob was from Kansas. He didn't have access to free medical care and must have been concerned. She patted his hand. "I've got you, Bob. Don't fret."

Bundling up, she went out and found the book. She set out looking for the errant employee. She understood a sick person not reporting in, but when the train was stalled and passengers were cold, all maintenance personnel should have shown up to assist.

Halfway down the train, she knocked on a staff door.

And pounded harder.

As she was beating at it, Chris entered the car.

"What's up?"

"Trying to rouse this character. I can't find him anywhere else. He must be in his room. He should be on duty."

"I've got it." Chris pulled a keycard from his pocket. "Jenny has Twyla doing something else. I'm checking every room. This is my last car." He swiped the key and opened the door.

Someone groaned.

Maddie stepped past Chris.

"Go away. I'm sick." The man in the bed waved weakly.

"I'm a nurse." She hurried to his side. There were two beds in the room. Both of them occupied. "Are you okay?" she asked the other man.

"No. Sick."

Neither man had a fever. They appeared to have food poisoning. She looked around the room. Empty food containers and dishes littered every surface, even the floor. She banked her anger. They probably poisoned themselves by eating unrefrigerated leftovers. "I'll get you something to treat this, and more blankets. You need to stay warm." She closed the door and headed for the car, where there was a small room that served as an emergency clinic. The meds she needed were there.

"Shouldn't they come to a heated car?" Chris followed her.

"For a short time, they'll be okay bundled up here. If this isn't food poisoning, we can't risk getting everyone else sick."

"Good call. I can find extra blankets for them."

She looked at him over her shoulder. His earlier animosity had lightened up. Was it permanent or temporary? She hoped for the former. "Thank you,

Chris. I appreciate the help. How many people are unaccounted for?" she asked in her nicest voice. "I'd like to be sure everyone is safe."

"With those two, we've got everyone. Jenny managed to find an actual paper copy of the passenger list."

She sighed. "Thank you, Chris. For everything."

He shrugged. "Just doing my job."

"No. You're going above and beyond. I never would have thought to check the engine. Thank heaven you did. You may have saved Bob's life."

Her phone rang. She yanked it out. "Hello."

Katie O'Connor

## Chapter Nine

Chris watched her expression change from concern to relief. She did have a very expressive face. She was churning with tension. He could almost see it. She had to be totally freaked out about their situation. But she kept going, kept working toward a solution.

"Yes. Thank you. We'll be ready." She disconnected and jumped around. "Yes. Yes. Yes. The helicopter is on its way! They'll be here in about half an hour."

"It's a good thing we passed out of the mountains."

"Yes. It is. I have to go get Bob ready."

"Mind if I tag along? I have to report to Jenny."

"Sure, but blankets and meds first."

With the two ill maintenance men taken care of, they hurried forward. Considering that Maddie was a good four or six inches shorter than he was, she made good time.

As they passed through occupied cars, she paused briefly to talk to staff and passengers. She reassured everyone that help was coming, and that there was enough propane to keep cooking and providing hot beverages. She encouraged the staff to be generous with snacks.

"What about wood for the fire?" an elderly lady asked.

"We have enough. And should we run out, we'll burn the chairs."

The old lady looked startled but impressed. "Won't the train company get upset?"

"My dear," Maddie patted the lady's mittened hand, "You worry about staying warm and I'll worry about the train company. I've got this handled."

"But you're just a nurse."

"She's more than a nurse," Chris piped up. "She's an organizational wizard and a representative of the train company. What she says goes."

A murmur went through the crowd and Maddie smiled her thanks at him. He hadn't lied. It was true. He'd seen her skills in action as they researched contestants, and now in getting the staff to pull together during the crisis.

"Who won the contest?" a man called out.

Chris groaned. Now was not the time.

"Great question." Maddie smiled at the speaker. "There will be a final announcement when we get to the Rocky Mountain House Depot. They're setting up a celebration that will be ready for us when we arrive." The celebration had been planned, but her people were now adding to it. Making sure nobody went hungry. There would be doctors there as well, to ensure nobody was injured.

People began peppering her with questions. Chris held up his hand and whistled. "Okay, everyone. We're safe at the moment. Help is on the way. We'll deal with your questions later. Cliff, behind the bar, knows where to find us in an emergency. Please stay calm. Think about the stories you'll be able to tell when you get home."

They pushed their way through the mumbling crowd. In the next car, which was blissfully empty, he said, "We're going to need to find a way to keep everyone calm. Got any ideas?"

She scratched her head through her pink toque. "Not really. All I know is that I'll be refunding people's money. At least a portion of it."

"Why? If nobody misses their ride home and nobody is injured, I don't see a reason. This was booked as a trip of a lifetime, right?"

"Yes, but..." She shook her head. "I'll worry about that later. I need to check in with the depot."

She made the call. She asked and answered a lot of questions. Her replies impressed him with their thoughtfulness. She didn't make any hasty decisions. She was genuinely concerned about the safety and well-being of her passengers.

Her joyous whoop startled him.

"Yes. Yes. Thank you. We'll be ready." After a bit more conversation, she hung up the phone. She danced a happy jig and threw her arms around him. "We're saved!"

He savored the hug for a moment. They had never gotten around to hugging, and she fit perfectly in his arms. Just as he'd imagined she would, only better.

Abruptly, she jumped back. "Sorry about that. I got excited."

"I noticed." He flashed a smile. "What's up?"

"Monique, my Rocky manager has a hundred snowmobiles headed our way. Each has a passenger sled. We can bundle everyone up and send them into town." She sobered. "Unfortunately, it will be days before we get a replacement engine or even someone to check this one out." She shrugged. "At least the people will be safe. Let's talk with Jenny and make an evacuation plan."

She headed forward, and he swore he heard her say, "Note to self: get a diesel generator for the train so we always have heat and lights." He banked a snicker. It was adorable how she talked to herself.

She stopped before they entered the forward observation car.

"What?" he nearly bumped into her back. "Are you okay?"

"No. Yes." She pivoted toward him. "Just pulling my crap together so I can get through this dumpster fire of a trip. This is not what I had planned."

"Nobody plans for disasters. We plan for the good."

"It was my responsibility to plan for all contingencies. I got wrapped up in the planning and the fun. I failed."

"I don't know about that," he said honestly. "It looks to me like you're pulling things together nicely. A helicopter for Bob. Rides for the passengers. A plan to deal with the issue should it happen again. You probably feel you're swimming upstream, but from where I stand, you're doing fine, all things considered."

She was. She didn't panic; wasn't throwing blame anywhere but at herself, and as near as he could tell, there was no way to predict engine failure and the cascading problems it caused.

They had several men go out into the early dawn and stomp down the snow in the adjacent field to create a path for the medics to reach the train easily.

A private helicopter landed in the adjacent field and after the nurse who came with it checked Bob over, they flew toward the Rocky Mountain House hospital. They stood in the windy field and watched it fly away. "That's a relief."

"It sure is. I was assuming STARS would come," Chris admitted.

"This was faster. I wanted him under a doctor's care as fast as possible. Not that Melvin wasn't great. He's a pediatrician, and I wanted a cardiac specialist." She shrugged expressively and turned back toward the train. "Maybe I need a doctor on the train like a cruise ship has a doctor. Something to consider. Maddie," she said to herself, "add 'research doctors' to your to-do list."

When the first snowmobiles arrived, they began loading the children and elderly first. Fortunately, the drivers had brought warm blankets and sleeping bags for their passengers, most of whom had warm jackets but not snow pants. In groups of two or three, they drove off toward town, snugly bundled up and safe.

"I'll stay behind," Maddie said. "There just isn't enough room for all of us. Go ahead, Chris. Take the last spot. I'll get them to send someone back for me. I'll be fine. The sun is warming everything up."

"No."

"Yes. I am your boss, and you'll do what I tell you." Her glare was impressive, but didn't sway his decision one bit.

"Fine. I quit."

She vibrated with anger, hard enough that he saw her shaking. "Chris..." Her tone was pure warning.

"If you think I'm going to leave you here alone for hours, you are sadly mistaken." He turned to the driver of the last machine. "Go ahead. We'll wait for the next one." The driver sped away and Chris turned back toward Maddie. "Let's go inside and warm up. I could use a hot drink."

"I could use a drink drink." She groaned. "Man, do I need a drink!"

She pulled out her phone and requested one more ride.

Inside, the car was chaos. Abandoned blankets and dishes lay everywhere. It looked exactly like it was, the remains of a disaster. But at least it was warm. In fact, with the fire burning brightly, it was nice enough he shed his jacket.

Maddie stood in the doorway, a blank look on her face.

"Come over here and get warm, Maddie."

She took two steps and picked up a coffee cup from the floor. Then another and another. She carried them to the bar, set them down, and began folding blankets with her back to him. She fumbled with her mittens, threw them on the floor with a grunt, and went back to folding.

"Maddie. Stop. Come and warm up. Please."

She kept folding, moving around the car, always with her back toward him.

"Maddie," he barked.

"What?" She whirled around and glared at him. Tears streamed down her cheeks. "I have to clean this mess up. You could help."

"Oh, honey. Folding blankets won't fix this mess." He strode toward her, stepping carefully over blankets and dishes strewn about the floor. He wrapped his arms around her. She leaned in, sobbing.

His stomach clenched and his heart ripped. She didn't deserve this pain. He rubbed her back and made soothing sounds until her sobs lessened.

"It's going to be okay. Our ride will be here soon. We'll join the others and have a party. We'll announce the winners."

She groaned and pulled away.

"I don't know who won. I don't even know if the last two groups finished their challenges. This is a disaster." She started pacing.

He pulled a leather loveseat closer to the fire and draped several blankets over it. Then he stoked the fire with the last wood in the firebox. Taking her by the shoulders, he led her to the couch and gently pushed her down.

He sat with her and covered them both with blankets before sliding his arm around her. He ignored the detritus all around them and focused on the tiny, unlit tree in the corner. This was Christmas. Christmas Eve, to be precise. It was a time of joy, or it should be.

A voice whispered that it was also the time of forgiveness and love.

Reality hit him like a smack to the face. He loved this woman. She was soft-hearted and strong. Loving, caring. She was funny and quirky.

"Chris?" her voice was barely a whisper and cracked on the single word. She swallowed hard.

"Yeah?"

"I'm sorry."

"This wasn't your fault." She had nothing to apologize for. The train's problems weren't her fault.

"No. Not that. I'm sorry I lied. I should have been upfront from the start. Or at least a lot sooner."

"Why'd you do it, Maddie? Why did you lie?"

"It's like I told you last night. Golly, was it only last night? People, so many people, have tried to steal my money. They pretended to care about me, to get close to me. I was worried you'd be the same. I should have known better. Three times, I had you investigated. Three times."

He laughed. "I figured you would have. And in truth, I tried to investigate you. You've hidden your identity well."

"Anyway. I'm sorry. More sorry than you could ever know."

He leaned his head over against hers. "It's okay."

"No, it isn't. My behavior was inexcusable. Especially after I learned about your past. The trouble is..." she sighed heavily. "The trouble is that I fell in love with you somewhere along the way. I just didn't believe what my heart was saying. My father was right. I'm an airhead that doesn't think things through."

"Your father said that? What kind of man does that?" He turned to look her in the eye. "Madeline Hayes, you are smart and kind. You aren't an airhead at all. You've got a good mind for business. Look what you've built with this train. It's all over the news that people want to book trips, especially at Christmas. Your idea is brilliant."

She looked up at him, hope shimmering in her tears. "Really?" she whispered.

"Really."

"Thank you." She was silent for a long time, but she didn't break their gazes apart. "Chris, I swear I'll never lie to you again. But there's one more thing..."

"What's that?"

"Can you kiss me? Just once, so I have the memory when we're far apart?"

"No, Maddie. I can't kiss you just once."

Tears brimmed in her eyes.

"I have to kiss you a thousand times. Every day for the rest of our lives. I love you, Maddie."

He swooped forward, pausing just long enough for her to object, though he knew she wouldn't. At the first touch of her lips, lightning rocked through him and his cells burst to life. Joy and elation shook him. He devoured her mouth. Tasting. Demanding. Giving. She pushed forward, urging him on with a desperation that matched his own.

Breathless, he leaned back. "Holy smokes. You pack a punch."

She laughed. "So do you." Looking up at him, she whispered, "More?"

Katie O'Connor

# Chapter Ten

The train station was rocking when they pulled up on the sled. It was a party that was in full swing. Reluctant to leave Chris's embrace now that she'd earned his trust back, she looked up at him. "I don't want to get off. I like cuddling you."

"Later. We have a party to attend, and winners to announce. This is going to floor everyone." He leaped off and stared down at her with the softest smile she'd ever seen.

Sweet cookies and cream. She loved this man.

"Do I look okay?" she asked, pulling off her toque and knowing she was a disaster.

"Beautiful."

She smiled so widely it hurt. "Liar. But thanks." She turned to their driver. "Keith, thanks so much for the ride. You literally saved our lives. Why don't you come in and join the party? Judging by the machines here, everyone else stayed. Come. Please be part of our celebration of life and Christmas."

"Thanks, but I need to get home to my family."

"Bring them along. The more the merrier. It's Christmas!" She shouted the last words. "Seriously, call them and have them join us. We owe you and your friends everything." She had already suggested via phone that the other rescuers bring their families along.

"Maybe I will." He climbed off and removed his helmet. "Thanks."

"Thank you."

She grasped Chris by the hand. Her heart thundered a million beats a minute. "Sheesh, my heart's going to explode. I'm so nervous."

"What's there to be nervous about? You don't have to admit you are the benefactor, just that you work for her or them."

"Good point." The man was brilliant. She popped up on her toes and kissed him. "Let's go."

She hadn't been to the building yet. She paused to study it. It was fashioned to look exactly like a turn-of-the-century depot, only bigger. It was draped with brightly lit evergreen swags that accentuated its light wood siding. The multi-paned windows glowed with light even in the daytime. It was exactly what she envisioned, right down to the full-length swinging doors. Pictures had not done it justice.

"You're stalling," Christ whispered, squeezing her hand.

"Savoring the moment." She tugged his hand, and they raced up the steps and through the doors and slammed into a gaiety of noise. Laughter, singing, dancing, dishes clattering. It was the most beautiful sound she'd ever heard...except for Chris confessing his love and forgiving her. Nothing beat that.

She shivered with delicious excitement.

A piercing whistle cut through the noise. "Here they are!"

The crowd roared and clapped and stamped their feet in welcome.

Jenny rushed over and hugged her.

"You're holding hands!"

"Yes. I'll tell you about it later." She couldn't wait to share her love with the woman who had become her best friend and who hadn't cared about her hidden identity or her money. Jenny led them to a podium and flipped on the mic.

"Ladies and gentlemen, your attention please!" The crowd quieted. "Our first business is serious. Bob Siffeldeen will make a full recovery. His heart attack is minor."

A cheer rose high and echoed off the rafters.

"Now, I present to you the Rocky Mountain Christmas Train's official judges, Madeline Hayes, and Christopher Watson. You probably don't recognize Chris in this form. You'll know him better as that cranky old man in a wheelchair."

"Hey," Chris grumbled lightly, making the crowd laugh again.

Jenny stepped back, and Maddie stepped forward. This was what she'd worked so hard for. She looked out over the crowd. Contestants and passengers mingled with staff, reporters, and bloggers. It was the perfect moment.

This was where she made up for all the times she'd been a nasty person or had treated other people like she was above them. This is what Nanna's money was meant for. It wasn't for high living. It was for helping others. If her parent's money did the same, it was just a bonus. A way to give back for her sheltered, privileged life.

"Merry Christmas, everyone."

"Merry Christmas!" they shouted back.

"Chris and I are here representing the Rocky Mountain Christmas Train, and we're going to announce the winning team." She waited for the rumble of approval to die down, even though she was over-excited to make the announcement. This was her dream.

"It's been an interesting twenty-four days. Especially this last one." The comment was met with chuckles. "Before we make the final announcement, can I have the following teams step forward, please? Team Yip, Team Rhyme and Dine, Team T-Rex, Team Paira Parkas, Team Triple Threat, Team Misty River, and Team Little Bear." She waited until they were all up front before continuing.

"Let's have a hand for these teams. Team Misty River and Team Litle Bear, I've been informed that you did indeed meet your challenges. You, and the rest of these teams went above and beyond to accomplish their goals. I want each and every contestant to know that I was impressed with your work. You can hold your heads high."

The crowd remained silent.

"The management of the Rocky Mountain Christmas Train, owned and operated by Rocky Mountain Rail is pleased to announce that these teams," she paused dramatically, "and all the other teams who remained in the contest and who were not disqualified for cheating, yes even those who tried and failed to meet their challenges, will all receive twenty-five thousand dollars for their charity of choice."

The crowd went insane.

Chris whistled, and they quieted down.

"Those teams with two different charities will be awarded twenty-five thousand dollars to each charity."

The crowd's excited murmur made her giddy. So many happy people. It was a thrill she hadn't imagined. "Merry Christmas, everyone. And may God bless you all." She flipped off the mic and stepped away from the podium.

Chris swung her into his arms and kissed her senseless. "I so misjudged you when I found out you lied. You have the biggest heart of anyone I've ever met. When did you decide to pay everyone?"

"On the ride here. It just seemed right, and I can afford it. Of course, next year might be a different story. Or a whole new contest idea." The idea made her heart soar almost as much as hugging Chris. "I love you," she whispered and kissed him again.

"Miss Maddie, Mr. Chris, are you getting married?" Chantal's excited voice broke into their kiss.

"Maybe?" Maddie said just as Chris said "Yes."

"Yay. Mama and Seth are getting married, too. It's my Christmas present."

"That's wonderful. Congratulations," she said to the happy couple who stood behind their daughter. "When's the big day?"

Joy laughed. "Boxing Day, and we'd love it if you two could stand up for us."

"Absolutely, we'd be honored." They'd done this. She and Chris had brought this family together!

They chatted for a few moments before Tracy and Rex pushed forward. "This is so incredible," Tracy said. "We can put a huge down payment on our studio. I'll teach dance, Rex will teach Karate. You've made both our dreams come true."

Rex kissed Tracy's cheek. "You've brought us together and that's the best Christmas gift ever. Thank you."

"I'm so happy for you both."

"Oh, there's Jenny. I need to talk to her." Tracy rushed off, leaving Rex behind.

Rex watched her go with a smile on his face. "She's amazing. Just so you know, I'm going to propose tomorrow and I'm pretty sure she'll say yes."

Chris gave him a man hug and they slapped each other's backs in celebration. "Well done, my friend. Well done."

"Thanks. I better go over there. She's waving to me. Thanks again."

"Wow. Two proposals and all I wanted to do was bring awareness to charities and help people smooth out their lives."

"That's a beautiful smile," Chris said, pressing his lips to her forehead. "Can I just say that I'm proud of you and of what you've done?"

"What we've done but yes, please say it."

He tickled her side.

"Oh, look," she said. "There's Bruce and he's holding hands with one of the paying customers. Oh, my goodness. I didn't know they were dating."

"So that's who it is. Bruce mentioned he was interested in someone the night we snuck into town for our date. They weren't dating then, but they look happy together."

"They sure do." She sighed happily.

He turned her to face him and waited until he had her full attention before speaking. "I love you, Maddie. I want to spend the rest of my life with you. Will you marry this poor private investigator and make him a lucky man?"

She tapped her finger on her lips like she was thinking, while inside her heart was screaming yes. "Will you stay on as my personal private investigator?"

"As long as I don't have to move to New York. It's a great place to visit, but I love Alberta."

She shook her head. "Well, I suppose I could accept that condition. Yes, Chris, I will marry you. Today, tomorrow, any day you want. I love you. You won the ticket to my heart."

Grinning, he swept her up in a kiss that sent her heart and soul soaring towards the future.

"Merry Christmas, Maddie."

Katie O'Connor

*Epilogue*

Curious to know the future of the contestants that you fell in love with?

**Team Rhyme and Dine**: Paige Chamberlain and Davyn Kayne:
She's sporting a sparkly ring on her left hand. She's given her notice at the Over Easy Diner and is moving to California to be with Davyn, whose career is soaring once again. Paige has already registered for some January classes to achieve her high school diploma. They couldn't be happier.

**Team Paira-Parkas**: Elspeth Mary Stone and John Stuart:
John plans to give Elspeth a ring later that evening on Christmas Eve at the Stone's ranch in Wolford, Alberta. John is going back to Jasper, Alberta, to resign from his firm. They're going to enjoy just being engaged until the New Year, when they'll start making decisions about wedding plans and their future.

**Team T-Rex**: Tracy McLeod and Rex Harrington:
On Christmas day, Tracy gives Rex the "Rat King" doll she bought from the Creston Farmers Market. Rex responds with a gift of his own, a simple diamond solitaire, and a proposal. Rex uses his winnings as a down payment on the dance studio that they will share to teach dance and martial arts to the local children.

Tracy honors her commitment and donates her winnings to the local hospital cancer treatment program to assist cancer patients with transport and lodging during their treatments.

**Team Yip**: Tess Burton and Dalton Wainwright:
Tess agrees to move back in with Dalton and his dog friend, Grace. She vows to help him overcome his phobias and become the man he's dreamed he could be. They'll also talk about children now that they've had the dog talk. Dalton eagerly accepts Tess and her dog into his life and his home.

**Team Triple Threat**: Joy Spencer and Seth Mathison:
Seth and Joy are married on Boxing Day with Chantal proudly standing as their flower girl while Maddie and Chris act as their witnesses. They'll live together in Alberta in a lovely house which Chantal helps them choose. That summer, Chantal is thrilled to learn that by next Christmas she'll have a sibling to play with. What they haven't told her is that she's getting two.

**Madeline Hayes and Christopher Watson**:
Maddie and Chris are married on New Year's Eve. Later that year, they'll have their first child, of many. The Rocky Mountain Christmas Train will continue to roll every Christmas with the benefactor remaining anonymous despite the media's continued attempts to determine who it is. The train itself will grow to be a popular luxury line and roll year-round filled with happy tourists. Jenny, Bruce, Twyla, Cliff, a fully recovered Bob, and many other staff return year after

year to help keep the charity contest on the rails, with some additions and upgrades the benefactor determined were necessary given the eventful 'last' stop.

Katie O'Connor

# Nanaimo Bars

## Ingredients:

- 1 cup butter, softened, divided into 2
- 5 tablespoons unsweetened cocoa powder
- ¼ cup white sugar
- 1 egg, beaten
- 1 ¾ cups graham cracker crumbs
- 1 cup flaked coconut
- ½ cup finely chopped almonds (Optional)
- 3 tablespoons heavy cream
- 2 tablespoons custard powder
- 2 cups confectioners' sugar
- 4 (1 ounce) squares semisweet baking chocolate
- 2 teaspoons butter

## Directions:

1. Gather ingredients.
2. Bottom Layer: In the top of a double boiler, or the microwave combine 1/2 cup softened butter, cocoa powder, and sugar. Stir occasionally until melted and smooth.
3. Beat in egg and stir until thick, 2 to 3 minutes.
4. Remove from the heat and mix in graham cracker crumbs, coconut, and almonds. Press into the bottom of an ungreased 8x8-inch pan. Optional: line pan with parchment. This allows you to top the entire tray of squares out onto a cutting board for faster slicing.
5. Middle Layer: Beat remaining 1/2 cup softened butter, heavy cream, and custard powder until light and fluffy. Mix in confectioners' sugar until smooth. Spread over the bottom layer in the pan. Chill to set.

6. While the second layer is chilling, melt semisweet chocolate and 2 teaspoons butter together in the microwave or over low heat. Be careful not to scorch the mixture.
7. Spread the chocolate-butter mixture over the chilled bars.
8. Let the chocolate harden before cutting into squares.
9. Optional: Once partially set, use a toothpick to draw the squares in the chocolate. This helps the chocolate stay intact when sliced.
10. Slice and enjoy.

# About Katie O'Connor

Best-selling author Katie O'Connor lives in Calgary, Alberta, Canada. She married her high school sweetheart and is living her happily ever after. She is the mother of two grown daughters and is extremely proud of her five grandchildren.

She is the founder of The Write Chicks, a private romance writers' group set up with the sole purpose of supporting each other's writing career. Currently, she is past president of the Calgary Association of the Romance Writers of America. In the past, she's been their secretary and has also served on the organizing committee for When Words Collide, a reader and writer conference in Calgary, Alberta. In 2025 she will be a Story Coach for the Alexandra Writer's Center Society in Calgary.

Katie's career path has been long and twisted, with most of her life devoted to her family. She's been a waitress, chambermaid, cashier, store manager, as well as a lab and X-ray technician. She's been a small business owner and is an avid quilter and crafter.

She's dabbled in writing since high school because something drives her to create stories. She swears it's impossible for her NOT to write. Unsatisfied with one genre, Katie writes contemporary romance, erotic romance, fantasy/paranormal romance, romantic suspense, and erotica.

## Katie O'Connor

She believes in all things magical, including dragons, fairies, UFOs, ghosts, and house pixies. But most of all she believes in love, romance, and hope.

## Where to Find Katie

Website: https://katieohwrites.com
Email: katie@katieohwrites.com
Mailchimp Signup: http://eepurl.com/Q2nRr
Facebook: http://www.facebook.com/katieohwrites
Bookbub: https://www.bookbub.com/profile/katie-o-connor
Instagram: https://www.instagram.com/katieohwrites/
Goodreads:
https://www.goodreads.com/author/show/5362469.Katie_O
_Connor

## *Books by Katie O'Connor*

***Coyote Creek***:
A Lesson in Love 1
A Heart Torn Apart 2
A Secret to Shatter 3
A Melody for Christmas 4
A Surrender so Sweet 5
A Place Called Home 6
A Love to Rebuild 7
Coming Home for Christmas 8
Coyote Creek Box Set 1
Coyote Creek Box Set 2

***Cherry Lake Fire Fighters:***
Sugar Cookie Kisses
Cappuccino Mugs and Fire Fighter Hugs

***A Silver Fox Christmas:***
Their Christmas Heart
Their Christmas Love
Their Perfect Christmas
A Silver Fox Christmas Box Set

***Hearts Haven:***
Running Home
Building Trust
Saving Grace
Heart's Haven Box Set

***Three Moon Falls:***
Fire Magic
Water Magic

Ticket to Her Heart

Earth Magic